ZERO DAY

BOOKS BY JAN THOMPSON

Binary Hackers (4 Books)
JanThompson.com/binary

Protector Sweethearts (6 Books)
JanThompson.com/protector

Defender Sweethearts (6 Books)
JanThompson.com/defender

Savannah Sweethearts (11 Books)
JanThompson.com/savannah

Vacation Sweethearts (8 Books)
JanThompson.com/vacation

Seaside Chapel (6 Books)
JanThompson.com/seaside

Keep up with Jan Thompson's book news:
JanThompson.com/newsletter

ZERO DAY

BINARY HACKERS BOOK 2

JAN THOMPSON

GEORGIA
PRESS

Zero Day (Binary Hackers Book 2)

Copyright © 2020 Jan Edttii Lim Thompson
Published by Georgia Press LLC
Author Website: JanThompson.com
Book News: JanThompson.com/newsletter

This book is a work of fiction. All characters, persons, places, events, and things either are the product of the author's active imagination or are used fictitiously.

Cover Design by Deranged Doctor Design

eBook ISBN 978-1-944188-59-7
Paperback ISBN 978-1-944188-62-7

To my Lord and Savior, Jesus Christ, who died on the cross to save me from my sins and rose again from the grave to give me eternal life in heaven.

For God so loved the world that He gave His only begotten Son, that whoever believes in Him should not perish but have everlasting life.
—John 3:16

ABOUT ZERO DAY
BINARY HACKERS BOOK 2

A maligned hacker.
A Mossad agent.
A mutual enemy.

No longer of any use to the governments who once coveted his cybercriminal mind, disgraced hacker

Kelvin Gallagher finds himself languishing in Prague while waiting for his enemies to find him and end his sufferings. Along comes a Mossad agent, once a friend, but now determined to take him home in a body bag...

Zero Day is book 2 in my **Binary Hackers** series of inspirational near-future cyberthrillers combining technothriller and romance. If you're looking for clean suspense without compromising faith, these books are for you.

I started writing *Zero Day* when I wondered what would happen to a hacker who straddles the fence between wanting to do what is right while doing all the wrong things. Whereas in *Zero Sum* (book 1), I explore the problems with cybernetic implants, *Zero Day* (book 2) takes us behind the scenes to the other side, to the people who made those implants for a nefarious purpose, and to the moral battles in their minds.

We met Kelvin in the first pages of *Zero Sum*, shortly before he was whisked away to parts unknown. In *Zero Day*, we pick up his story some months afterwards.

The prisoner awaits...

Down and out and waiting to die, mercenary hacker Kelvin Gallagher regrets betraying his homeland. Rejected by everyone, Kelvin has no choice but dig deeper into the dark hole into which he has fallen.

He remembers his ex-employers at Binary Systems, Inc., who have given him a job when nobody else dared. Are Cayson Yang and Leland Yang-Joule more moral than he is? He thinks not. Aren't they all working for money?

Yeah, life is worth more than money. Kelvin knows that, but it's too late. Way too late as he sits in a rat-infested rundown building in Old Prague, fearful and in anguish.

The executioner comes...

As an act of revenge, former Mossad agent Yona Epstein tracks down the American traitor who led her mentor to the slaughterhouse. It makes Yona angry that Kelvin used to be a friend, back when they worked together in a project.

When Yona uncovers Kelvin's hideout in Europe, she realizes she isn't the only one who wants Kelvin dead. That makes her pause.

To kill or not to kill...

When Kelvin explains to Yona his version of the cybercrime nightmare of his own making, several events don't match up with what Yona has been told by her associates.

Is Kelvin innocent after all? Should Yona delay the execution until she finds out what is going on? Or proceed based on the information she already has? She trusts her sources, doesn't she?

Before Yona can decide on how to deal with Kelvin, enemies close in as their past catches up to them.

Zero Day (Binary Hackers Book 2)
JanThompson.com/zeroday

Binary Hackers
JanThompson.com/binary

Book News from Jan Thompson:
JanThompson.com/newsletter

ZERO DAY

CHAPTER ONE

Tuna and shrimp for dinner tonight wouldn't have smelled this bad to Kelvin Gallagher if it hadn't been from a can he shared with Mordecai the stray cat who came to his fourth-floor hideout every couple of nights to kill rats for him.

This hadn't been how Kelvin had envisioned his last days on earth, sitting on death row in a condemned building in Old Town Prague, waiting for God to take him to Heaven, where he expected to feast at the table with the King of Kings and Lord of Lords.

Meanwhile, cat food.

Kelvin gagged.

He pushed the can away, and as if on cue, His

Royal Catness appeared through the crack in the broken wooden slats in the window, trotting toward the heavenly smell.

"Have it all." Again. "Don't worry about me. I need to lose weight, anyway."

It was dusk outside. It felt like dusk. But he dared not peek out of the window, as if doing so would hasten his own demise.

Someone would see him.

He reminded himself that the elderly grandmother two doors down was the only person who knew he was hiding in this building—only because she had fed him dried pork and leftover pickled vegetables every now and then. And because she allowed him to take a quick shower in her house once a week to conserve water.

Tereza's heart of gold could get her killed.

I must leave. But where do I go?

No passport. No work visa. No money.

He was now an illegal alien in the Czech Republic, dumped here by rogue Federal Security Service of the Russian Federation agents, who had wrestled him out of Aspasia's hands. They had no use for him anymore, since MedusaNet was all but shut down. So they dropped him off in Prague to protect themselves from liability.

Yeah, liability.

Those former FSB agents were more like mercenaries, thinking they would earn a whole lot more American dollars freelancing than if they had worked as salaried employees of the Russian government.

Ironically, they hadn't left him here in the pursuit of money. They had left him here for assassins to find him—if Aspasia didn't find him first.

Kelvin berated himself repeatedly for not asking those people for at least a fake passport and some *koruny české* or maybe even euro banknotes.

"I'm all alone. I have to get out of this myself." Kelvin wrapped his arms around his bended knees and leaned back against the wall, paint peeling off here and there. "Where are You, God? I need a miracle. I need a miracle."

Why didn't God stop him from leaving Atlanta eight months before? If he had remained in town, his employers at Binary Systems would have found him.

What choice did he have, honestly? There he was that fateful day in September, walking around the convention floor, snacking and picking up free merchandise, when out of the corner of his eye he spotted Aspasia walking toward the YottaFlops booth that he and his employer, Cayson Yang, had set up.

He had wanted to warn Cayson, but he saw the woman spray some sort of liquid in Cayson's face. Then he watched his boss go down just before she stabbed the side of his head with some sort of device.

Which he later found out had activated the cybernetic implant in Cayson's head.

She had looked up from the floor and stared straight at Kelvin.

Kelvin remembered dropping the 3D-printed bobblehead doll of himself, and running for his life. It didn't help that he had worn a bright yellow T-shirt.

Aspasia caught up with him in no time, with those FSB agents not too far behind her.

And here I am.

Well, yeah, by way of Moscow, but that was the part Kelvin didn't want to think about.

"Meow."

Looking past the cat, Kelvin saw the empty can on the old wooden floor.

"That's all I got, buddy." Kelvin shuffled his way to his makeshift bed at a corner of the room.

His bed was a pile of old, torn blankets he had salvaged from the neighborhood dumpsters. On top of it was a plastic bag he had stuffed with rags. He puffed it up and put his head on it.

Mordecai came over and sat on the blanket with him. He cleaned his gray and white-speckled fur.

"When I leave this place, I'll take you with me, okay?" Kelvin tapped his head. The cat purred. "That is, if I physically leave. If I die, then I can't keep my word, you know."

The gray cat settled down at an edge of Kelvin's blanket and began to clean his paws.

Kelvin felt thirsty. He stared at the crack in the ceiling. He worried that the ceiling would cave in, though ironically it would usher in a faster death for him.

Was death the only way out?

He wasn't sure.

He tried to pray, but no words came to his mind or mouth. He had been a churchgoer back in Atlanta, in his younger carefree days when he wanted to do everything right in the eyes of God.

No eventuality like this ever crossed his mind.

No, his goal was to buy his mother a house on the beach on Tybee Island, and provide her with a personal chef and housekeeper. She could spend her days reading books on the balcony overlooking the Atlantic Ocean.

That had been his goal.

Until her lung cancer worsened, and Kelvin

needed money quickly before time ran out. She never went into remission, and three months after the chemotherapy, she asked to be taken off treatment so that she could die in peace at home.

That had been when Aspasia had shown up, offering Kelvin a job behind the job. All he had to do was plant back doors into their network they were constructing for Birmingham Bytes, a British company with international clients.

Kelvin dusted off his hacking skills and joined the covert team. It was a win-win. He could moonlight the project and still keep his day job as a system administrator at Binary Systems.

He would walk away with a cool ten million dollars.

Easy money.

Yeah.

The cat snuggled next to him, and Kelvin closed his eyes.

He saw his mother laughing and smiling, walking at the ocean's edge on Tybee Island against a backdrop of the five-million-dollar oceanfront home he had bought for her. He still had another five million to splurge on her.

He remembered how his mother kissed him on the forehead in their last days together, just as she had done all his life whenever he had been a good boy. Little did she know that he had sold his soul to buy her the mansion.

And two months later, she passed away.

The beachfront house, paid for in cash through an overseas company, became vacant after Mother died. Kelvin didn't want to stay there.

Soon thereafter, Birmingham Bytes went out of business and its assets were sold to pay off their debts. Little did anyone know that MedusaNet would be sold to Molyneux, a terrorist at large who had robbed everybody from MI-6 to the CIA and everyone in between.

The other shoe dropped when Kelvin learned that the network he had been hired to test and protect was none other than MedusaNet.

He'd had no choice but to do what Aspasia wanted. She had threatened to kill his mother. Even though she was dying of cancer, Kelvin wanted to give her the best end-of-life care ever.

After Aspasia let him go home for his mother's funeral, he sold the beach house, breaking even, and tried to return the money to Aspasia. She wouldn't take it.

She simply wouldn't take it back.

If he had...

If only...

Nah.

Hindsight could not save him now. "I reaped what I sowed."

Do not be deceived, God is not mocked; for whatever a man sows, that he will also reap.

Galatians 6:7 couldn't help him now. The deed had been done.

In fact, Aspasia had threatened him with death if he went to the authorities.

There was no way Kelvin could go to the police at all. He would end up implicating himself. That company, Birmingham Bytes, no longer existed. It had served its purpose, and now was absorbed into the MedusaNet systems.

Too late.

"Everything is too late." Kelvin sighed as rain fell on the roof.

He opened his eyes and jumped out of bed. He gathered up a few cups and a can, opened the window slightly, and placed the chipped cups and dented can on the windowsill. Rainwater dripped into the cups.

"Thank You, God, for water." Kelvin stuck his head out, and washed his hair in the rain.

The night was dark and he could not see

beyond the dim moonlight. He prayed that nobody saw his face out here.

Outside his windows were rows of tiled roofs—red during the day—stretching all the way to the Vltava River, or at least to the street in front of it.

The rain beat down noisily, and he could not hear the city tonight. The music festival had just started a day or two ago. Sometimes during the day, he could hear music and the crowd, though he could not see Charles Bridge from here, five blocks away.

Music, festivities, food...

Kelvin's stomach rumbled. He reached out for one of the dirty cups. There was already half an inch of water in there. He poured it into another cup. And did so with the other cups until he had one cup of water.

"Diet dinner." He chuckled.

CHAPTER TWO

Two days after she quit the Israeli Secret Intelligence Service, Mossad assassin Yona Epstein found herself in Prague, gliding up a flight of stone stairs, hugging the shadows of darkness under cracked windows blaring a cacophony of classical and pop.

Every now and then voices—television?—interspersed with "Everybody Wants to Rule the World," that eighties song from the British pop band, Tears for Fears.

Yona's gloved fingers tracked the uneven walls of a row of buildings, sweat forming on her palm. May wasn't the time of year for her to wear Kevlar under her black shirt and hooded denim jacket, but she had to blend in with the Mozart crowd at the music festival a block away while waiting for the locator software to work—although her Kevlar-reinforced backpack would have given her away had anyone taken the time to study her movements.

It had taken over ninety minutes, but it worked. And just in time too, as the rain that fell heavily across Prague finally slowed down. When Yona had received Kelvin Gallagher's location, she was on the wrong side of Charles Bridge, but made a mad dash across the river from Malá Strana to Old Town.

If Mossad found out that she had paid some people to hack into the *Metsada* field network in Prague in order to track the USA Central Intelligence Agency operatives hunting down Kelvin, the unit commander would come looking for her. She'd have a lot to answer for, especially when she was no longer a *katsa*—the field agent she had dreamed of becoming since high school and had achieved before she was thirty.

And now all that went out the window because she had decided not to rest until she tracked down Kelvin, the hacker responsible for putting her mentor in the crosshairs of the terrorist, Molyneux.

Kelvin had handed a veteran Mossad agent over to the terrorists, and the Mossad wasn't going to do anything about it.

Or had he?

Yona hadn't been a hundred percent sure that Kelvin was complicit in the situation until Reuel pointed all fingers at him.

Yona had no reason not to believe Reuel. Next to Issachar, Reuel was the only other person in the entire Mossad whom Yona trusted with her life.

Sure, Molyneux had been captured alive and was now standing trial at the International Criminal Court in The Hague in the Netherlands, but she had left an anonymous successor who had rebuilt their international underground computer network—with huge help from a team that included Kelvin, her quarry tonight.

That was why Yona had to leave Mossad.

Why she had to do this alone.

A dark alley opened up at the top of the stairs, just as the last drops of rain fell. Yona kept her hood on as she stepped carefully on the cobblestones, her black combat boots supporting her heels on the uneven surface.

The alley smelled of ammonia and sewage and rain. Yona held her breath half the time as she made her way through the alley.

Suddenly she pulled back, and splayed her palms against the wet wall behind her.

Shadows crossed the other end of the small alley. One, two, three shadows.

Probably nothing.

Yona drew a deep breath.

She inched forward.

The shadows ahead of her slowed down.

She did too.

They were going in the same direction as she was.

It could be a simple coincidence.

Yona tried not to worry. Prague was crowded today due to the music festival. Concertgoers were all over the place, walking about, eating, singing, dancing in the streets. All day and all night.

Those were probably just—

Someone glanced her way.

Yona froze.

She could not backtrack. The alley might be narrow and dark, but it was between two tall walls. There was literally no place to hide.

Suddenly someone groaned. A second person spoke in Czech. Something about getting another drink. They laughed.

The couple appeared in the dim light, staggering and singing out of tune.

The shadows ahead shook their heads and kept walking.

Thank You, God.

Yona followed the couple out onto the street and sidewalk. From the corner of her eye, she saw three figures step toward a door. Under the streetlights, two of them pushed through the heavy wooden door.

They disappeared.

Yona's eyes widened as she looked at her watch. That was the same location she was heading to. An abandoned building. Nobody lived there—except maybe Kelvin.

Who were those people?

She waited a few more seconds before she made her move.

And wished she hadn't come alone.

CHAPTER THREE

Having covered her nose and mouth with a black mask which she had brought with her, Yona climbed the stairs in the musty stairwell, the Sig Sauer she had picked up from a local contact in her right hand. Personally, she preferred a Glock, but that was all Issachar's friend had available. He wanted Kelvin dead as much as Yona did, so the Sig was free.

Yona's intel said Kelvin was on the fourth floor of this abandoned building. She wished the rain had continued to fall because the natural noise-cancellation would have masked her presence.

She felt exposed, but the musty stairwell was her fastest way up. Her intel also said there was an elevator somewhere, but it was on the other end of the building. Besides, she had no time to test if the elevator even worked in this once-office complex that had seen better days some fifty-odd years before.

A piece of cement broke off from the edge of a step under Yona's combat boots. She held her breath and froze.

She couldn't hear anything else but the silent sound of something foreboding, as though she was walking into a trap.

What trap, exactly?

What did she care?

This mission of hers had effectively ended her illustrious career at the Mossad. No retirement check, no bonus, no advancement, no commendation. It was all over the moment she quit her job and flew to Europe to hunt down Kelvin.

And here he was, holed up in this condemned building.

On the third floor, she heard something.

Fist on flesh? Fist on bone?

Accompanied by a muffled groan.

Was someone being tortured? Kelvin torturing someone else?

The truth remained that Yona still had a hard time believing that Kelvin had sold out Issachar. To whom, exactly? To Molyneux and her now defunct organization? To her successor? To the owners of MedusaNet?

What good was a dead Issachar to those terrorists?

He would be worth his weight in diamonds if he had been alive.

Yona sniffled.

Stepping across the dark floor, and then up the final flight of stairs, Yona wondered if she was in the right state of mind to be here.

Maybe that was why even Issachar's best friend in Prague had warned her to grieve first before taking vengeance.

"How long must I grieve?" Yona remembered asking.

"At least six months. Three years, if needed." Reuel had always been wise, but he knew his deceased friend's protégé was impatient. "But if you must go now, let me help you."

And help her, he did.

Yona arrived in Prague a week before on a tourist visa, with tickets to whatever classical concerts were happening this month. She even stayed through an entire Antoine Dvořák concerto performed by the Czech Philharmonic Orchestra, even though she preferred Béla Bartók, although not as much as her parents. They would have loved to be in the city at this time.

However, this wasn't a family vacation.

This was a mission of vengeance.

Before she left the hotel, Reuel had warned her again not to do it.

"You're emotional right now because you're sad that Issachar is dead."

Reuel's words peppered her mind as she climbed the last flight of stairs.

How dare he recite Deuteronomy 32:35 to her? Now she couldn't get it out of her head.

Vengeance is Mine, and recompense;
Their foot shall slip in due time;
For the day of their calamity is at hand,
And the things to come hasten upon them.

"Child, vengeance belongs to the Lord," Reuel reminded her.

Yona hated being called a child.

She was thirty-four years old. What was Reuel thinking, insulting her like that?

A smell of decayed fish assaulted her nose. What on earth?

She realized then that her mask was useless. However, it hid her face from anyone who could identify her and send word to Mossad about her unofficial visit to Prague to meet with Reuel, who had been tracking Kelvin for her, even as he protested all along the way.

In her head now, Yona could hear Reuel read another Bible verse. The same verse over and over. Yona didn't like how he used Romans 12:19 against her.

> *Beloved, do not avenge yourselves, but rather give place to wrath; for it is written, "Vengeance is Mine, I will repay," says the Lord.*

Yona knew she had to be reminded not to take matters into her own hands, but to give that prerogative to God.

It was God's Word to her, was it not? Delivered through Reuel as the eighty-eight-year-old man implored and begged her to call off her pursuit of the hacker.

But Issachar...

She blinked.

Maybe Reuel had given her good advice. She wasn't in the right emotional state to be meting out vengeance and vigilante justice—

No.

Kelvin must die.

Tonight.

She heard a woman's voice coming from a room down the hallway. The door was partially hanging off the frame. Inside was dark, except for what seemed to be flashlights or lamps.

Her voice sounded familiar.

Very familiar.

She had heard it before on a mission with Issachar.

Before she could make a guess, something brushed past her calf. She was surrounded by darkness, so she couldn't tell what it was. It felt like a feather duster or maybe something else just as soft.

Or she was merely imagining things.

Then she heard a quiet meow, the sound going away from her.

A cat in the night.

CHAPTER FOUR

One more blow to the head, and Kelvin fell over on his side, hitting his head on the wooden floor. With his arms tied behind his back and his ankles duct-taped together, he was unable to speak through the dirty cloth taut across his mouth.

His head spun.

Aspasia was saying something, but he couldn't decipher it. It was in English, yes, but what was she saying?

Mumble, mumble.

Kelvin closed his eyes. This was how his life would end. Here in an old city where he had no family, no friends, no one. He had been waiting for weeks for a bevy of assassins to come get him.

Unfortunately, he wasn't as popular as he had thought.

The only person who had come to the door in the last two months was Aspasia. She wasn't even looking for him per se. All she wanted was information on Ulysses. For that, she was willing to kill, but only to get to her goals.

Maybe nobody else cared if Kelvin was dead or alive.

Perhaps it would have been wiser for him to turn himself over to the CIA. They should be around here somewhere. Weren't they everywhere?

"Get him up." Aspasia's voice again.

Strong arms lifted his shoulders and put him back on his bended knees. He felt like that samurai warrior about to be beheaded.

At least Aspasia wasn't asking him to commit hara-kiri.

Kelvin tuned out Aspasia, and began to pray for forgiveness from God.

I know what got me here, Lord. I need... Help me, Lord. I need You now. If You think I should get out of here, then please hurry. If You think this is the end of me on earth, please let it be painless.

"When was the last time you communicated with Ulysses?" Aspasia asked.

Make it painless.

Kelvin couldn't return the ten million dollars that Aspasia had paid him for the work on Medusa-Net. It was too late. The money was tainted, his reputation ruined, and now his life was at stake.

> *For the love of money is a root of all kinds of evil, for which some have strayed from the faith in their greediness, and pierced themselves through with many sorrows.*

I Timothy 6:10 offered no comfort to Kelvin.

He was finished.

Tears pooled in his eyes.

Thank God his mother wasn't here to see this cesspool he was swimming in.

He closed his eyes and let the tears wash over his face. They stung his cheeks a little. He felt his own warm tears flow down his chin and neck, and onto his shirt.

A sudden flash of bright light startled him. Had he been shot?

The light was so bright he couldn't open his eyes. Weirdly, it made him almost rejoice, as if he were in a passageway out of this sorry world.

Suddenly he heard a familiar voice calling his name.

He hadn't heard the voice in four years.

It can't be.

~

K elvin was a bag of bones, perhaps as heavy as the rucksack Yona had to carry in basic training a long time ago when she had been on Parris Island, South Carolina. That seemed like eons ago, way before her parents decided to move to Jerusalem and become Israeli citizens.

After Yona finished eight years with the US Marines, she joined her parents in Israel and found herself recruited by the Mossad.

Five years later, she had betrayed her newly adopted country.

All because of this man.

Yona dragged Kelvin by his collar out of the room until his ragged shirt ripped.

Behind them, CIA Protective Agent Dario de la Cruz gone rogue, and Dmitri's men—mostly former FSB—were cleaning the floor with Aspasia's men.

As for that elusive snake, she had escaped by leaping out of the window before Yona could catch her. She'd missed Aspasia's boots by a hair's breadth.

Yona watched Aspasia parachute four floors down to the rained-out dark alley below. Never looking back, the woman once known as Meta Hoon vanished into the night.

Yona counted five of Aspasia's men against Dario and Dmitri. She jumped in, but Dario brushed her away.

"Get Kelvin out of here!" Dario yelled at her.

And so she did.

The hallway was dimly lit, but most of the lights were out, so Yona could not see into the dark distance. Somewhere at the end of the hallway, there should be an elevator.

In front of them was the top of the stairs. Four flights down.

"Can you walk?" Yona asked Kelvin.

He didn't answer.

Passed out, but not dead.

Could she drag him down the stairs?

The fighting continued behind her. She didn't trust the CIA or FSB—retired or otherwise.

She should have expected Dario to arrive soon after she did. She had beaten them to the building by a few minutes, but former agents of the FSB?

Why would Dario work with them?

Granted, they were Dmitri's men. Dmitri was now a naturalized American citizen living on a farm in North Georgia. He'd had very little contact with the outside world—until last year, when he had been called in to help Binary Systems, Kelvin's employer.

Kelvin groaned. One eye opened.

"Can you get up?" Without waiting for an answer, Yona pulled him to his feet and dragged him to the stairs.

"Wait—Yona?" Kelvin rubbed his eyes. "Why are you here?"

To kill you.

"Talk later, dude. Right now, we need to get you out of here before we both get killed."

"Where's Aspasia?"

Yona shrugged. She pushed Kelvin forward. He limped down the stairs, but said nothing about whether that was his route of choice or if they should have taken the elevator.

"Walk faster." Yona knew the stairway was dark, but they had to get out of there.

"I can't see where I'm going." Kelvin pointed into the abyss. "I don't usually come down these stairs at night."

Ping!

Yona spun around. She heard it again.

Someone's shooting at us!

"Whoa." Kelvin must have realized it now

because he lowered his voice. He picked up his pace.

He still had his senses about him, Yona thought.

They ran down the stairs in the low light, guided by a dim lamp on the ground floor. Kelvin was in front. Yona picked up the rear, praying that nobody would shoot at her head, where she had no protection.

She heard a ping again, and this time the pressure was on her backpack.

The noise of boots on the stairs became louder.

"Hurry!" Kelvin barked.

"You're telling me?" Yona held onto the handrail with one hand as she took two steps at once, knowing that the crumbling cement and tiles on the old floor weren't reliable.

In the daylight, this was probably some glorious stairway.

In the night, it was a death trap.

"One more floor." Kelvin leapt onto a landing.

Yona heard footfalls and boots on the stairs right behind them.

Without warning, something sudden and hard hit Yona's backpack and she lurched forward directly into Kelvin. He lost his footing, and went down.

They toppled on each other, twisting, turning,

and tripping down the stairs. Jack and Jill tumbled down the last flight of stairs, shoes kicking each other's face, and Yona trying not to scream, as they performed their impromptu flight of fancy all the way down—

Landing on top of something squishy.

And headless.

CHAPTER FIVE

G unfire.

    "Run!" Dario's voice came from above. "Get up, you two!"

More gunfire.

Someone running down the stairs.

Kelvin pushed himself off the dead body. Glanced over to see Yona sitting up on the harlequin floor, holding her head.

Is she real?

"Yona?" He helped her to her feet, but realized that something was wrong with his elbow. He touched it. No bones sticking out. But it started to hurt just as something sticky flowed down his arm.

She groaned. "I'm going to be black and blue in the morning."

"Anything broken?" Kelvin peeled back. Didn't want to touch her.

Three years before, he would have tried. In fact, he had asked her out on a date one day when they had a lull in their work. However, Yona was one of those people who kept her work separate from her personal life.

She had said no.

Kelvin understood why, though. Yona was a busy observer in Project Pericarp, and Kelvin was busy keeping the systems running so that Binary Systems and Ulysses could do their work.

Kelvin dared not ask her again. Not even for coffee. Or tea. Whatever her preference.

Someone jumped off the last step. Dario de la Cruz, whose path Binary Systems had crossed many times. He was alone, which told Kelvin this wasn't a CIA operation.

The only time Dario wandered off the beaten path was to rescue Binary Systems hackers, which Kelvin used to be—before he took over the system administration of the network.

"Everyone okay?" Dario asked, glancing back.

Yona nodded before she let out a hiss. "My ankle."

"We'll take a look later. We need to get out of

here." Dario turned on a small flashlight. Pointed to the front door.

"Where's your entourage?" Yona limped.

Dario drew a deep breath. "We'll talk later. Let's get to the safe house."

As Dario talked on the phone, Kelvin avoided looking at Yona. He had nothing to give her now. And he had no dignity to keep for himself.

His life was ruined. It might as well have been over.

They stepped outside onto the sidewalk, with only a distant traffic light providing low visibility.

"This way." Dario pointed.

They rounded a corner, and a black van pulled up to the curb. The door opened.

Leland Yang-Joule yelled from the driver's seat. "Get in!"

Dario helped Yona, who continued to limp. Then he swept her up in her arms and carried her into the van.

Kelvin's heart fell through the floor. He knew he could never be Dario. Brave and buff.

Dario put Yona in the back seat.

Kelvin entered the van on his own strength. He tried not to make eye contact, but he knew he had to say something to Leland, the co-owner of Binary Systems, Inc., his employer. Technically, he answered to Cayson Yang, Leland's cousin and Chief Operating Officer, but Leland could fire Kelvin at any time as well.

Kelvin scooted to the other end of the bench seat, as Dario got in the van and closed the door.

"Put on your safety belt." Dario made Kelvin buckle in. "We don't want you to die now that we've rescued you from Aspasia."

"What does Aspasia want?" Leland asked from the driver's seat.

Nobody answered her.

"Let me see your wrists," Dario said.

"What?" Kelvin saw the large cable tie in Dario's hand. "You don't trust me?"

"I don't want anyone to accuse us of not taking a modicum of prevention." Dario tied up Kelvin's wrists.

"Kel," Leland said quietly as she drove in traffic.

The way she said it sounded like she was disappointed.

Kelvin didn't reply. Too ashamed, he was.

"He's pouting," Dario said. "Let him be."

Dario didn't seem to show his feelings. Then again, his job at the CIA as a protector agent didn't require a show of personal opinions. In this face, Kelvin figured Dario's job was to keep him alive.

That meant the CIA wanted something. Maybe Kelvin could use it as a leverage to get reduced sentencing. He was quite sure he was going to get court-martialed for what he had done. He wasn't sure they'd pick and choose what they wanted to charge him with. And he couldn't afford a great lawyer.

Sitting in the back, Yona said not a word.

It was better for her not to say anything than to go against him. He had plenty of enemies already, thank you.

Then again, Kelvin hadn't worked with Mossad in four years. Why was a Mossad agent here?

Kelvin had so many questions. He leaned back on the headrest. If Yona wanted to slice his throat, this would be the time for her to do it.

Kelvin waited.

Nothing happened.

"What does Aspasia want?" Leland asked again.

Instead of answering, Dario scolded her. "I told you to stay in the safe house."

"The internet connection was bad. We took the van together closer to the building."

A realization struck Kelvin. "Why did you come for me?"

"You were waiting to die, and we can't let that happen to you." Dario handed out hand wipes.

Hand wipes? Kelvin had to laugh.

"Who were those people who came with you?" Kelvin said. "Are they Dmitri's men?"

"Were. I'll need to talk to Dmitri about that. I don't think they work for him if they tried to kill you and Yona." Dario turned to Yona. "Speaking of whom, why are you in Prague?"

"Same reason you are." Yona's voice was even, giving nothing away.

That was the thing with her. Kelvin could never read her feelings.

"And what reason might that be?" Dario asked.

"You tell me." Yona stood her ground.

"All I can say is that the CIA wants Kelvin alive, and apparently Aspasia wants him dead."

Kelvin shifted in his seat. "Aspasia doesn't want me dead."

"Had a gun pointed at your head, didn't she?"

"It was only to scare me."

"Into doing what?"

"She has been searching the world over for Ulysses."

"Isn't that interesting?" Leland glanced at the rearview mirror. "We haven't heard that name in a while."

Dario told Kelvin to stay still as he ran a portable scanner over him, head to toe.

"What are you doing?" Kelvin asked.

"Shhh." Dario read the results on an iPad.

Kelvin waited.

"Okay. He's clear," Dario said. "No chips."

Kelvin flinched. "You thought maybe the FSB injected me with something before they let me go?"

Dario shrugged. "Who knows."

"Then anyone could have found me." Kelvin sagged into his seat. "How did you find me?"

No one replied.

"I guess one of you will tell me later." Kelvin spent the rest of the drive staring out the window. The city of Prague didn't sleep. People were still walking about, sitting at outdoor restaurants, strolling by the river. The van went along the river, but Kelvin didn't ask where they were taking him.

Implicitly, he trusted Leland and her cousin, Cayson. They would do their best to make sure no harm came to him.

"Leland?" Kelvin's voice was low, but apparently Leland heard him. "I'm sorry."

"You better be," Leland replied. "You're going to get us all killed, and you'll lose your job because Binary Systems will cease to exist. Then what? Do you have a twenty-year plan before you decide to work on MedusaNet behind our back?"

That woman is blunt.

"I'm sorry." It was all Kelvin could say at this point, though there was nothing to hide from the CIA or Mossad. They had all read his story. "I know I'm going to jail."

"You'd rather die," Dario added.

Kelvin nodded. "Kill me now."

"Can't. We need you to help us find the people behind MedusaNet."

"Is the network..."

"We shut it down with the kill switch in Cayson's head," Leland said.

Kelvin flinched. *That must've been painful.* "I had nothing to do with that."

"Fortunately for you, everyone wants you dead," Dario said. "Which means you do have something they all want, and therefore it makes sense for us to keep you alive until we figure out what's wrong. Maybe you can tell us what you know and save us all some time and sanity."

"I don't know what they want." Kelvin didn't say that *they* meant many people. If he were to list his enemies, he would need to use all fingers and toes to count.

"We'll find out," Dario said.

It could only mean one thing. They wanted to use him as bait. Kelvin wasn't sure if it was a good idea, although it wasn't necessarily bad. After all, he had thought he was going to die, so if a short extension of his life could bring the criminals to justice, maybe it would be worth it.

He had nothing left to live for.

CHAPTER SIX

"I'm worried about my cat," Kelvin said as Dario ushered him into the safe house.

Yona limped along. Her sprained ankle was still hurting a bit. She was sure she'd feel it in the morning.

She watched the conversation with her jaw agape. Right now, she wanted to shake Kelvin awake and make him smell the coffee of reality.

His life—and that of everyone else affected by his error in judgment—were all at stake. The last thing he should be worried about was a cat.

"He's a stray, I know," Kelvin added. "But Tereza and I both feed him."

"Tereza?" Yona asked.

"She lives next door and sometimes gives me food and a place to shower."

Yona didn't know what to think about that.

"She's a widow with grandkids." Kelvin looked intently at Yona, as if he felt a need to explain the other woman in his life.

Yona let it pass.

"Mordecai was with me when nobody else was," Kelvin continued. "God sent the cat to keep me company at the lowest point of my life."

"The lowest point of your life is when you're dead." Dario cut off the cable tie around Kelvin's wrist. "Do not leave this house."

"And go where?" Kelvin asked.

They were inside the foyer of the safe house somewhere in Malá Strana on this new town side of the Vltava River. Dario locked and bolted the door behind them.

Leland had disappeared somewhere.

Dario's job was to take Kelvin and Yona to their rooms.

In the morning they would regroup at breakfast and figure out everything, if that was even possible.

"Tereza in the next building is pushing ninety. She's been feeding Mordecai scraps of food, but she's dirt poor herself," Kelvin went on. "Her son had been paying her mortgage, but he has been late several times."

"That's not your problem, is it?" Dario asked.

"If she loses the house, the cat has nowhere to go."

"I'm assuming he had been fending for himself before you showed up."

Kelvin nodded. "He's a street cat."

"Where do you plan to take him? With you to jail?" Dario's sharp tongue sliced and diced the evening air.

"I can ask someone to take care of him until I'm released."

"Like who?"

"I don't know." Kelvin shrugged. His shoulders slacked. He looked defeated.

Yona drew a deep breath. "When this is over, I will check on the cat for you. What does he like to eat?"

Kelvin stared at Yona for the longest time, making her uncomfortable.

Yeah, she had just offered to check on the cat.

"Mackerel," Kelvin said. "If you can't find that, tuna or shrimp will do."

"Does he eat out of a can?"

"I put it in a bowl for him."

"Okay." She didn't know what else to say, so

she turned to Dario. "I need to shower and rest. Please show me to my room."

"How's your ankle?" Dario asked.

"Still bad. Do you have some stretch gauze or something? I may need to wrap it up."

"I'll see what I can find in the first-aid kit." Dario pointed to the stairs. "You sure you can climb up?"

"Yeah. You don't need to carry me." Yona limped up slowly. "Where's Leland?"

"Checking on something."

"What do you do for food?"

"Thinking of breakfast already?" Dario smiled. "We'll have to cook. The safe house is low budget and doesn't come with a personal chef. Also, no swimming pools or hot jacuzzi. Lukewarm showers for everyone. Trust me, you want to be first in the shower because there will not be enough hot water to go around. And do your own laundry. No towel service."

"What kind of a hotel is this?" Yona laughed. Their small talk took her mind off her ankle.

"The one-star kind." Dario's voice softened.

Yona wondered if he was recalling the memories of his fellow CIA officers who had perished in the line of duty. All that was left of them was one star each on the Memorial Wall at Langley. Not a word would be spoken about their service to the country and the world.

Yona also wondered how the tides would have turned if it had been eight of Dario's fellow CIA officers killed instead of Mossad agents. Would Dario feel more urgency?

Here they were, getting rest and sleep, and breakfast.

Meanwhile, the families of lost Mossad agents were still grieving back in Israel.

And Yona was still grieving the death of her mentor. Issachar must not die in vain.

Her eyes met Kelvin's. For a femtosecond, she wanted to attack him and wring his neck.

However, moments before, she had offered to rescue his cat.

This was no way for an assassin to operate.

Have I lost my edge?

Upstairs, Yona's bedroom was on the opposite end of the hallway from Kelvin.

Just as well. Yona hoped and prayed that she would not decide to stop weighing all the pros and cons, and avenge Issachar already.

Still, the logical mind in her had begun to ask questions.

The logical mind in her had been raising flags all day about Kelvin's complicity in Issachar's death. Yona found herself wondering about the extent of his crimes.

Was Kelvin altogether guilty? Partially guilty?

Trapped in a mess of his own doing? Caught in a mess not of his own doing?

Or somewhere in between all the above?

The doubt came when Dario's men turned on him back at the building.

Wait a minute.

That was what Dario said. His only supporting fact was that people had shot at Yona and Kelvin as they came down the stairs. Who were those people? It had been too dark to see.

Yona replayed the entire scene in her mind.

She and Kelvin had gone down the stairs first.

Then shots were fired at them.

After that, Dario came to their rescue.

Somehow, coming down the stairs behind them, he hadn't been shot at all. Well, that was because he came after the gunmen.

At this point, Yona assumed they were all men because Dario had called them Dmitri's men.

"Let me know if you need anything," Dario said as he handed Yona the key outside her bedroom. "Leland's going to bring you some spare clothes. She always overpacks."

"Who overpacks?" Leland came up the stairs.

"Isn't it a good thing? We have guests." Dario chuckled, and left Yona with Leland while he and Kelvin walked to the other end of the hallway.

"I don't know if these fit you, but they're my exercise sweatpants, and they have an elastic waist." Leland handed Yona a pair of hot pink sweatpants, and a hot tangerine sweatshirt.

"You wear these?"

Leland nodded. "Well, I'm usually indoors in my home gym, so nobody sees. I don't wear neon outside. I much prefer to blend in."

"Me too. Thank you."

"There's a laundry room on the other side of the stairs if you want to wash your clothes tonight. The dryer works okay but you'll probably need to go two rounds if you want your clothes to dry properly."

Yona wondered why they would need to do laundry if they would be here for only a few days. Unless this was Leland's base of operation.

"I didn't realize Binary Systems works in Europe," Yona said.

"We don't have an office here."

To Yona, Leland seemed to have evaded her question. It told her that Binary Systems moved around in Europe.

The safe house meant their current project was classified.

"How long have you been in Prague?" Yona recalled Reuel telling her that Dario was in town two weeks before.

"Long enough. I missed Cayson's engagement party." Leland had cleverly deflected her question yet again, and Yona noticed it.

"Engagement?"

"To Stella Evans."

"Oh. I thought they were only close friends in Project Pericarp. I had no idea..."

All Yona remembered was that while the Mossad had sent her to observe the project, the FBI sent Agent Evans to keep an eye on the hackers as well. There were also a few people from NSA undercover, but Yona hadn't paid much attention to them.

"Suffice to say that in the yearlong project, lots of relationships formed." Leland drew a deep breath. She lowered her voice. "Look, I don't know what your relationship is with Kelvin, but I wondered why you were in town. Were you trying to protect him from someone? Maybe we can work together if our goals intersect."

Protect? It had been the opposite, but now

wasn't the time for a confession. Yona had to find out more about what was going on.

"I came here to get some information on who might have wanted my mentor, Issachar, murdered." It was the truth.

Even though Yona had jumped to the conclusion that Kelvin was blood-thirsty guilty, she had done so due to the intel that Reuel had given her.

Speaking of whom, she'd better call him. He'd want to know if she had dealt with her prey.

She had a burner phone, untraceable. It wouldn't lead anyone to their safe house if she called Reuel—she should at least text him.

"Until we know more, let's keep everything to ourselves," Leland said. "We've already seen that Dmitri's men can't be trusted. We'll not even contact him until we find out what's going on."

"Is Dmitri in on this?"

"I hope not." Leland's voice cracked. "Dmitri is my former mentor, back in my early hacker days."

"Is that why you're a hands-on COO? Dmitri had always been on the field even though he would have done as much behind a desk. His style rubbed off on you?"

"Once a hacker, always a hacker." Leland chuckled.

"Same for Kelvin, isn't it?" Yona replied. "He

started out a hacker. Why did Binary Systems make him a system administrator?"

"He was burning out and needed a change of pace. I'm not saying that being a sys admin is easier, but Kel thought he could do it." Leland started to leave, but she had more to say. "It was easier than having to interview and screen new employees."

"What happened to your previous system administrator?"

"He died suddenly. We found him unresponsive in the machine room."

"Oh."

"No warning, no telltale signs. His heart just gave out. It was a shame. He was only thirty-seven." Leland sighed. "After that sort of situation, you can see that it would be hard for Binary Systems to advertise an open position."

"Could be, if there's a matter of perception. Will Kelvin be turned over to the CIA?" Once he was in the custody of the CIA, Yona was sure she could not get her hands on him anymore.

She had prepared herself for this, but today's fiasco had raised too many questions.

Leland was unexpectedly quiet. Then: "Does the Mossad want Kelvin?"

"For questioning." It was all Yona dared to say.

"About?"

"About the events leading to the death of one of our Mossad agents—one week before he was supposed to retire."

"I'm sorry. You're close to him."

"I worked with him for years. He was like a father to me."

"That's how Dmitri is—except he's like a grandpa to me," Leland said. "If our projects are related, we could save time working together."

"So what's going to happen to Kelvin?" Yona asked as casually as she could.

"Dario locked him in his room. Tomorrow, we'll hand him over to the US Embassy to be extradited to the States."

"Why tomorrow?"

Leland seemed to hesitate. "Well, because we need him to do something for us. Once we turn him over, he goes into the court system, and we can't get to him except through a lawyer."

"But he... The EU would want him, not to mention the International Court."

"He's American and he broke our laws too."

"And the laws of Israel and the EU."

"To be honest, I don't know. All I know is that we found him first."

Yona looked at the ceiling. "How safe is this safe house?"

"It's CIA."

Yona could tell her stories of how Mossad had discovered CIA safe houses. If Mossad could, who was to say that Molyneux's successor couldn't?

Leland's eyebrows rose. "You know something we don't?"

"FSB put Kelvin in Prague."

"We checked, remember? No tracker. No GPS."

"I don't trust them."

"Neither do I. Dario is surely on it. Don't worry."

"Speaking of Dario, he was going to look for some stretch gauze for my sprained ankle."

"Oh?" Leland looked around. Neither of them had seen Dario since he locked Kelvin's bedroom door. "I think he went to bed. I'll go find some for you."

"Thank you. In the morning will do. I'm going to my room." Yona stepped back. "I better turn in. I've had a long day. I need to shower, read my Bible app, and get some sleep."

Leland nodded. "All right. See you in the morning. Breakfast is at eight o'clock. Dario is making cereal and he doesn't like people to be late."

"Cereal?"

"Yeah. It's his specialty."

"No eggs?"

"There are some eggs and bacon in the fridge, but you don't want Dario to cook. He'll set fire to the kitchen." Leland laughed all the way down the stairs.

Yona glanced down the hallway. Her observation skills must have been slacking. She didn't recall seeing him come back this way after showing Kelvin his bedroom. Maybe Dario's bedroom was on the other side of the hallway. Maybe he was closer to Kelvin to keep an eye on him.

Kelvin was now prized for the knowledge inside his head.

Everyone wanted a piece of him, including Aspasia. Why hadn't Aspasia killed Kelvin?

Until they waded to the bottom of this mess, Yona had no choice but to tag along and see what was going on before she carried out her mission.

In other words, don't try to kill him off prematurely.

CHAPTER SEVEN

K elvin tossed and turned in his bed for half the night. He felt guilty for sleeping on a comfortable mattress. This was no punishment for his many sins.

He felt clean after the long, hot shower. He had washed his hair umpteen times and scrubbed his feet. Then he brushed his teeth several times, as if once wasn't enough. Trying to make up for his two months off the grid.

It could have been longer had the FSB not retained him until they had exhausted all their questioning.

It was unusual that they had not implanted him with a tracker. That could only mean one thing: they had dropped him off to die.

"Hardly comforting that they have no use for me anymore," Kelvin said to no one.

Perhaps it was time for him to confess everything to Leland. She would understand his predicament, why he had done what he did.

Then again, regardless of Leland's compassion, Kelvin was going to jail.

For how long, though?

He could handle a few years, maybe.

Kelvin closed his eyes. Too tired to sleep. Too stressed to dream.

Stressed? How could he feel stressed if he was protected by Dario and his non-team?

He was sure reinforcements would come soon. Probably not from Dmitri. His men had turned on them. Nearly gotten Kelvin and Dario killed. And Yona.

Yona Epstein.

Why was she here?

What did she want from him?

Kelvin could hear water running down pipes. He ventured to guess it was probably the second-floor washing machine. They had taken turns washing their clothes tonight.

Who had woken up at this time to put in another load?

Leland?

She sometimes stayed up all night.

Kelvin heard the clothes dryer buzzer go off. Another load finished. If they didn't fold the clothes now, they would be all wrinkled in the morning.

Clink.

Kelvin stilled. What was that?

It couldn't have been the dryer because it had just stopped running. Besides, what would sound like metal against metal?

Kelvin had always prided himself for having sharp hearing. God had made him that way. He could hear very well—better than everyone in his family, with the exception of the family dog.

That single clinking sound...

Kelvin threw the covers off, leapt out of the bed, and tiptoed to his door to make sure it was locked. Then he crawled back into the bed and prayed.

This was supposed to be his first peaceful night—

A commotion began outside his door. It sounded like people fighting. Pounding at one another.

He heard male and female voices.

Kelvin started to shake. First, it was his hands. Then his legs. Then his entire body shook.

I'd rather be back in my abandoned building, please!

Someone knocked on the door. Keys turned.

Kelvin couldn't move. He was stuck under the blanket. He tried to lift his arms, but nothing moved.

He was frozen in place.

The door opened.

"Come on, Kelvin!" Dario shook his head. "Let's go!"

Dario strong-armed Kelvin. He fell out of bed. He couldn't get his legs to work.

"Let go of the blanket," Dario ordered. "We'll get you another one. Right now, they're trying to kill us."

The dim light from the hallway streamed into the room. Standing there at the door, Yona was in a sweatshirt and a pair of sweatpants. And carrying two weapons in her hands.

"Upstairs, you said?" Yona talked to Dario. She had all but ignored Kelvin.

Kelvin felt so small.

So useless.

So worthless.

He wanted to cry.

His life had hit rock bottom and there was no

way out. Everywhere he went, the smell of death had followed him and lingered all around him.

"I'm sorry," Kelvin said to Yona.

She didn't reply.

"Where's Leland?"

"Waiting for us on the roof." Dario pushed Kelvin forward.

They climbed the last flight of stairs at the end of the hallway. The door opened to a flat rooftop, where a helicopter waited.

Standing on the helipad, Leland was motioning for them to hurry. Kelvin saw how Yona was still limping, and he slowed down for her.

When they reached the chopper, Kelvin and Yona packed in like sardines in the back seats. In the front seats, Dario took the controls, and Leland sat in the passenger seat.

Everyone put on their headsets and the chopper lifted off into the night.

Suddenly Leland tossed Yona a large cable tie. "Put them on him."

"What?" Kelvin couldn't believe what he was hearing on his headset.

"Make sure he doesn't jump out!" Leland said.

Yona tied Kelvin's wrists together.

"Enjoy the ride," she said.

The night view of Prague below them made Kelvin feel like a tourist, but his heart wasn't in the sightseeing. He prayed again to ask God to forgive him.

It was starting to get real to him.

He wished he had never taken the ten million dollars from Aspasia.

He could have enjoyed this tremendous view.

Instead, this could be the last flight of his life.

CHAPTER EIGHT

The last place Yona expected to find a hacker hangout was near a golf resort some thirty minutes outside of Prague. However, their helicopter fit in with the millionaire and billionaire crowd who flew there to enjoy life on the course, even if they might not be the best golfers.

If Yona had thought they were going to mingle with the young, rich, and famous, she was wrong. As soon as all four of them exited the helicopter, a black van appeared, and they hopped in.

Only four of them were heading south, with Yona and Kelvin sitting on the bench seat behind Dario and Leland.

Kelvin hadn't protested when Dario tied up his

wrists with a giant cable tie. He seemed resigned to the fact that he had been caught and would end up standing trial.

Yona figured that if Kelvin had a good lawyer, they might be able to shave years off his sentence. If he offered to help the US government or EU, he might even further reduce his years behind bars.

It was two o'clock in the morning, and Yona was wide awake. Who wouldn't be? The ride was too bumpy.

She looked at Dario, driving the van. Whenever he turned toward Leland, Yona could see the bags under his eyes. He looked like he hadn't had enough sleep. His hair was disheveled, and his chin looked rough, as though he would need a shave in a matter of hours. He didn't speak a word.

In the front passenger seat again, Leland was texting furiously. "No, no. I told you. We're not going to the embassy."

Leland didn't say which embassy, but Yona knew they basically had three choices. Israeli was out of the question because she was here without authorization. Russian wouldn't be considered because the FSB had clearly infiltrated the ranks of Dmitri's security force.

The only embassy left with any possibility was

American—all the way back where they had come from, on the other side of the river in Malá Strana.

"Why not the US Embassy?" Yona asked after Leland put away her phone.

"I think we have a mole in the CIA or at the Embassy," Leland replied bluntly. "Nobody else knew we had Kelvin in the safe house. They gave us a twenty-four-hour window to do what we need Kelvin to do."

"What did you want him to do?" Yona asked.

"Kelvin knows." It was all Leland said.

Yona waited for someone to say something.

"They want me to help them get Ulysses," Kelvin told her. "However, we don't know if he's in charge of MedusaNet now."

"The situation is fluid," Dario said.

"If we get too close to Ulysses, we will all die," Kelvin warned them.

"Weren't you waiting to die back in Prague?" Yona blurted before she regretted it. She didn't mean that precisely. Yet the irony of her presence here was to end Kelvin's life.

Now all she wanted was an explanation. *Why did you cause Issachar to die, Kelvin? What has he done to you to deserve death?*

"Let's calm down and sort it out tomorrow." Dario yawned. "How far away is this place?"

Leland shrugged. "We'll find out when we get there."

"I don't know, Leland. This would be the third safe house?" Dario made a face. "I'm suddenly having trust issues. Maybe we should find our own place."

Kelvin buried his face in his hands. "It's all my fault. I'm so sorry."

"You're sorry the devil made you do it?" Without waiting for an answer from Kelvin, Dario turned to Yona. "Mossad has contacts in Prague."

Yona didn't respond. It seemed to her that Dario already knew the answer. He was fishing for something else.

"Can they help us?" Dario asked.

"I don't know."

"Because you quit your job, didn't you? You came here without authorization or funding."

Wow. Dario knew.

Whenever the streetlights appeared outside the van windows, Yona could see three pairs of eyes staring at her inside the van.

Then they turned their attention to the elephant in the car.

"When Binary Systems worked on Medusa-Net, we didn't know that it was going to be sold to Molyneux," Leland said. "However, two years later, the British company went under and MedusaNet suddenly had a new owner. You knew about the sale, Kel. Why didn't you say anything?"

"Ten million dollars says he didn't have to tell anyone," Dario replied.

Kelvin groaned. "My mother was in her last days on earth. There was no way Binary Systems could pay me that much for three months of work."

"Was that when you took a month off?" Leland asked. "Mental health sabbatical?"

"I'm sorry I couldn't tell you what I was up to. Aspasia threatened to kill my mother." When no one replied, Kelvin said more. "I'm so sorry."

"Sorry? Will that bring back Vivek, Danika, and Jamal?" Leland's voice was harsh. "You put us, our company, our reputation, our lives on the line. We nearly lost Cayson."

"I had no idea Aspasia was going to put implants in their heads."

"You escaped. How?"

"They needed me to maintain the network. Well, actually, I led the team that did it."

Yona was still listening. And recording the whole thing on her phone without anyone's knowledge. They'd sort out the legal ramifications later. Or they'd thank her for the foresight.

"You got names?" Dario asked.

"In a secret safe. If I have to make a deal, that's my insurance to get a reduced sentence."

"Fair enough. Continue."

"I worked on the system for a month, and then remotely for the next six months." Kelvin slowed down now, as if measuring his words.

"Didn't you say three months?" Yona asked.

"The project ran late."

"As with most software projects," Leland added. "What were your specs?"

"They wanted MedusaNet upgraded into a military grade network."

Leland shook his head. "And you did it for ten million dollars. How many lives did you sacrifice?"

"I have no idea. I told you. I did it for the money. When I found out who Molyneux was..." Kelvin choked. "Believe me, I tried to undo my work. Failing that, I tried to insert back doors so we could go back in and shut it down."

"We?" Leland asked.

"We, Binary Systems. USA. FBI. INTERPOL. Mossad. Whoever. The good side." Kelvin drew a deep breath. "I failed, Leland. I failed."

"You didn't fail," Leland reminded him. "We used the kill switch in Cayson's implant to knock out MedusaNet."

"We—my team and I—designed another virus—

a Plan B, so to speak, just in case the kill switch didn't work. It was never planted. I got caught in the middle of installing that."

"By Molyneux?"

"No. By some dude working on implants. Neon. He was in Ulysses's cybernetics division, but we had played chess together online. Somehow, he found out what I was doing. It must've slipped out of my mouth when I was blabbering."

"And yet he helped you."

"He wasn't going to, but it turned out that he was an informant for the Mossad." Kelvin looked at Yona.

Yona perked up when she heard Mossad mentioned, but Mossad had informants all over the world. She didn't know anyone by the name Neon, but if Issachar were alive, he would know who worked with informants inside Molyneux's organization.

"Why don't you find out who handled Neon?" Leland asked Dario.

Dario nodded. "It would be easier if Yona asked someone."

"I no longer work there," Yona said.

"Early retirement. Were you forced?" Dario asked.

"That's irrelevant to this. Why don't we hear

the rest of what Kelvin has to say?" Yona decided there was no point editing out that part of the conversation from the recorder.

In fact, because she no longer worked for the Mossad, she had more freedom to make her own calls.

Speaking of calls, she wondered if she should contact Reuel. The seasoned Mossad agent, semi-retired, might also know who handled Neon—if they could get his real name.

"What's Neon's real name?" Yona asked.

"That's the thing. He's dead. He got run over by a truck while he was crossing the street. After that, I knew I wasn't safe." Kelvin sighed. "I wish I had never bought Mother the big house."

"You could have rented," Dario said. "They have beachfront properties all along the coast."

"Where were you when I needed a financial advisor?" Kelvin asked. "Too late now, anyhow. I sold the house, tried to return the money to Aspasia, but she wouldn't take it."

"When was that?"

"A few months before I saw Aspasia at the convention talking to Cayson." Kelvin recalled having a good time going from booth to booth and collecting free merchandise. "When I saw her splash something on Cayson's face and he went down, I was like, what on earth?"

"You ran, but you didn't get far. Aspasia was after you."

"And she's still after me."

"One wonders why," Yona finally spoke. She didn't want to sound ignorant.

"I'm sure she found out that I put the kill switch in MedusaNet. However, I don't know who put it into Cayson's head. It can't be Neon because he's dead. Maybe his Mossad handler found someone else. Who could have done it?"

"Ulysses?" Dario guessed. "The grandmaster hacker himself."

Kelvin shook his head. "I'm not sure. The entire time I was in Prague and while I was working remotely, Aspasia never mentioned Ulysses."

"She did the day she activated Cayson's implant at the convention," Leland said.

"Did she? Maybe they had a falling-out?"

CHAPTER NINE

Almost three hours after they began driving slowly south, they arrived in Český Krumlov, a city still within the country of the Czech Republic. Kelvin had no idea why this city was chosen, but he only asked for a bed to sleep in.

And sleep he did, like a baby.

By the time he woke up, brushed his teeth, showered, and lost all sense of time of day, he wandered downstairs and found the other three people congregating in the living room.

Behind the couches and armchairs, a sliver of light came in through the windows.

"What time is it?" Kelvin asked.

"We already had dinner."

"Dinner?" Kelvin was surprised. "I haven't had a good night's sleep in a very long time."

"You slept all day." Leland pointed to a hallway. "There's plenty of ham and cheese in the fridge. You can make yourself a sandwich if you want."

"I'm assuming there's bread."

"You assumed correctly. No pita or tortilla. It's wheat, but nobody's sure if it's organic. It was already in the fridge when we got here this morning —last night."

"Who put it in there?"

"Probably Slash2Hack." It didn't seem to bother Leland that she had disclosed the name of one of her hacker friends who had been helping them with the case.

"Do I know her?" Kelvin asked.

"Him. And no, you don't. He changes names every few months."

Kelvin looked around. No place to sit in the small living room.

Yona stood up and limped out of the living room. Kelvin followed her.

"I'm not going to the kitchen," Yona said.

"A minute of your time?"

Yona seemed to mull it over. "We can go to the kitchen if you need to make a sandwich."

"Is there soup?"

"I don't know."

"What did you eat?"

"I didn't. I had a baked potato for lunch."

"Show me where the kitchen is, and I'll make you a sandwich," Kelvin offered.

"Sure. Just don't put poison in it." Yona laughed.

Why is she like that?

Kelvin didn't remember much about their meeting four years ago. Yona had been an observer, shadowing her mentor, Issachar.

Sometimes he wondered if Issachar was Neon's handler. Neon's killer was never found, as far as Kelvin knew.

Kelvin followed Yona down a narrow hallway. To one side was a row of arches, some of which led to another sitting area and a courtyard.

The kitchen was also small, but it had been updated some time ago.

"Ham and cheese?" Kelvin washed his hands.

"Anything. Shall I toast the bread?" Yona asked.

They spent at least ten minutes looking for a toaster. When they found it, it was unusable. Rusty inside and gunky, like someone had put different types of stuff in it.

Kelvin had to wash his hands again.

Yona sat on a barstool, amused.

Kelvin found a frying pan, melted butter in it, and toasted several slices of bread.

"I want to apologize," Kelvin said, flipping bread. He turned down the stove. "If there's anything I can do to help you, let me know."

"I'm looking for Issachar's killer."

"First, I have to know who Issachar was."

Yona explained, but all Kelvin could hear was her voice. It was soft, calm, unhurried, and had a tinge of an accent to it.

"Don't you think that you could have more resources on hand if you stayed in Mossad?" Kelvin asked.

"They've stopped all investigations."

"Why?"

"I don't know. Other murders are more pressing, I suppose. We have many cold cases."

Yona cut the ham in thick slices. She didn't ask Kelvin if he wanted thin slices instead. She just cut it the way she wanted and handed it to him.

He didn't care. He lightly browned the ham in the pan, and then slid it on top of a piece of bread. He put a slice of cheese on it, and then slapped another slice of bread on top. He flipped it and waited until the cheese was slightly melted.

"How many do you want?" Kelvin asked.

"Let's start with one. Make yourself one, and then we'll see if we want more."

"Okay."

"Would you like something to drink?" Yona opened the refrigerator. "Water, water, everywhere."

"Some cold water will be fine."

Kelvin dished out Yona's ham and cheese sandwich, cut it into two triangles, and placed it in front of Yona.

She didn't touch it.

"You want to split that?" Kelvin asked. "Quality control?"

Yona chuckled. "Sure. I was thinking that I'm not hungry and I don't know why."

"Anxious about something?" Kelvin placed a napkin near Yona's plate.

"About everything, really. Questioning everything."

"Do you regret leaving the Mossad to come out here, hunting for ghosts?"

Yona seemed surprised by the question.

"You came here to Prague—Czech Republic— to find the person responsible for your mentor's death, and you think it's me."

Silence across the table.

Total silence.

Kelvin figured he had pegged her.

"We're investigating all possibilities," Yona said.

Kelvin realized she had said *we*, but decided not to correct her. On the drive here, she had said she no longer worked at Mossad. So who were *we* exactly?

"How did you know I was in Prague?" Kelvin asked instead.

"I followed leads." Yona still hadn't touched her sandwich. "What were you doing in Prague?"

"I was waiting to die." It was the truth. "Ironically, I'm glad I didn't die. I wanted you to know, most of all, that I had nothing to do with any deaths in Mossad. Not directly, as far as I know. I mostly work with FSB who also wanted Molyneux."

"You worked for everyone, didn't you? You worked for Binary Systems, but the pay wasn't good enough. So you moonlighted with Aspasia, ended up working on MedusaNet, regretted doing it, and tried to undo your handiwork."

"My team and I succeeded, didn't we? Only I didn't know it worked because we installed it on the old MedusaNet, and it was one-sided. Now I know Neon—or someone else—carried through installing the switch."

"Someone put it in Cayson's head." Leland

stood at the door of the kitchen. "I was wondering what was going on in here."

"Yona thinks I had something to do with Issachar's death." Kelvin drank some water. "Tell her I have nothing to do with it."

Leland placed both hands on the countertop. "I don't know who fed you the information, but I've been in contact with the Mossad, and the trail for Issachar leads toward Molyneux, not Kelvin."

"He's going to jail and you're taking his side?" Yona got off the barstool. "I'm not hungry. Good night."

Kelvin watched Yona go. "She didn't eat her sandwich, and it's my fault."

"Bad dinner table conversation?" Leland found a piece of plastic wrap for Kelvin to wrap up the grilled cheese.

It would probably be soggy the next day, but Kelvin had made it for Yona.

"It's my fault," he kept saying.

"Normally, I would tell you to stop it already." Leland watched Kelvin put Yona's sandwich in the fridge. "But I have to agree with you. Many of these things are your fault."

"Why didn't Dario shackle me or something? I shouldn't be allowed to roam free."

"Are you though? Try leaving this house and see what Dario will do to you." Leland didn't laugh.

"I thought you were my...uh... Am I still employed at Binary Systems?" Kelvin wasn't sure why he even asked.

"Technically, you're AWOL."

"Absent without official leave. Great."

"And you're going to help us find the new people behind MedusaNet and make sure that network never resurrects itself."

Kelvin put his now-cold sandwich into the microwave. "In exchange for a lighter sentence, I hope."

"That's for a judge to decide, but I'm hoping so." Leland finished the bottled water and asked where the recycling bin was. When she found out there was none, she had no choice but to throw the empty bottle into the trash can. "Meanwhile, we have work to do."

"Where, though?"

"That's a good question. Tonight, we stay here, and then we'll have to move again."

"You know Aspasia will try to find us."

Leland nodded. "Dario's working on it. He's calling in favors."

"Favor from God is what I need right now."

"Don't we all, Kel? Don't we all?"

CHAPTER TEN

Yona had no idea how she went from sleeping in a single bed in the safe house in Český Krumlov to lying down sideways on some cold floor with her ankles and wrists tied up.

Her sprained ankle was throbbing something fierce. There was nothing she could do to alleviate the pain except pray for relief.

She didn't know where she was, but she heard airplane propellers whirring and aviation mechanics talking whenever a door opened. They were chatting in Czech, which Yona could identify but not speak.

She knew it was concrete beneath her because it felt cool under her arm and legs.

Otherwise, she was in utter darkness.

Was she alone?

Her gagged mouth prevented her from asking for help.

She tried to recall what had happened, but her mind was blank. She remembered getting upset with Kelvin in the kitchen. She went upstairs to brush her teeth and wash her face.

She texted Reuel on a secure line.

He didn't reply.

Then she fell asleep fully clothed on top of the comforter, her Sig Sauer in her backpack leaning against the side of the bed.

Next thing she knew, she woke up here.

How?

A large door screeched open. Light filled the giant room, casting shadows. A small group of people walked toward her.

Yona was right. This was a hangar, but more accurately, the back end of a hangar, where the mechanics kept spare engines and parts. No wonder she had heard mechanics talking nearby.

She heard a groan.

It was Kelvin. He was also tied up and gagged. He rolled to his side. Groaned again.

Where were the others? Leland? Dario? Were they held elsewhere?

The crowd parted, and Yona gasped.

Reuel?

~

"Isn't it always the case that your enemy is the one you least expected?" Reuel hobbled to an armchair that someone brought for him to sit in.

Kelvin made a face, and Yona wished he hadn't. It showed that Kelvin was affected by Reuel's words.

The elderly man motioned for someone to remove the bandanna around Yona's mouth.

"Nothing to say?" Reuel asked.

"I've never considered you my enemy." Yona chose her words carefully.

"Why would you say that? You think I'm too old?" Reuel chuckled. "I never pegged you to be the discriminating sort, Yona."

Something was wrong. In spite of Reuel's confession, Yona didn't believe he was the apex predator.

She wanted to think that someone like Ulysses might be pulling Reuel's strings. Ulysses was dead, wasn't he? Everyone thought so—except Aspasia. That poor thing believed the love of her life was still alive.

"What do you want from us?" Kelvin asked.

Totally the wrong question. Yet Yona understood that he was trying to help their situation.

"You'll see." Reuel turned to Yona. "You looked perplexed."

"You knew all along where Kelvin was hiding," Yona said. "Why didn't you go get him yourself?"

Reuel shrugged. "We figured it was easier to let you deal with Aspasia."

We.

There it was.

Yona knew she was right. Reuel wasn't in charge. Whose mouthpiece was he?

"What do you want from us?" Yona glanced at Kelvin.

Reuel didn't respond. Instead, he motioned for his people to take Kelvin away.

"Where are you taking him?" Yona asked, half-expecting him to ignore her second question.

Reuel waited until Kelvin was out of sight. "You and I need to talk."

Yona felt as though she was about to explode in words she'd regret later. There was nothing for them talk about if Reuel had taken them here by force. Drugged and all tied up? Those were no signs of friendship.

"How did we get here?" Yona asked as calmly as possible.

"I know you're angry."

Don't show emotions. "How did we get here?"

Intertwined in that question was Yona's other question: Were Leland and Dario doing fine?

"Let's just say we fumigated the entire building, put everyone to sleep, and carried you and Kelvin out of your bedrooms." Reuel seemed pleased that he had made it sound easy.

Truth be told, a CIA safe house wasn't that easily penetrable. Details, details. Yona was sure Reuel knew someone on the inside. Who?

"Just Kelvin and me? You killed the rest of the people in the house?"

"No need. We only want you and Kelvin."

"I appreciate your economy."

Reuel bowed his head slightly. "I aim to please."

"Why though? I've always been a friend to you. Both Issachar and I trusted you." Suddenly aware of what could have been a possibility, Yona found herself at a loss for words.

Could Reuel have killed Issachar? Over what?

"My old friend was always too trusting," Reuel said. "It's too bad he taught you the same. If you'd been more cunning..."

"I wouldn't be here today, tied up and sitting on the floor like this."

Reuel shrugged. "Like I said, we need to talk."

There was nothing Yona wanted to talk about with him. She would need more proof, but it was becoming clear to her who the traitor was.

All this time she had blamed Kelvin based on the evidence that Reuel had fed her.

Who blew Issachar's cover? Kelvin.

Who led to his death? Kelvin.

Who deserved the blame? Kelvin.

Who should die for this? Kelvin.

All lies. Lies!

"I thought you were on our side," Yona said.

"I'm on my own side." Reuel smiled.

Yona prayed for God to forgive her for listening to the wrong people.

Thank God for Dario and Leland!

They had stepped in just in time to prevent Yona from making an irreversible mistake.

A cloud of reasonable doubt hovered over Issachar's death.

Yona would have to start all over again with her investigation. At least now she had more evidence, yet not enough. She needed to find out what was really going on.

"All right. What do you want to talk about?" Yona asked.

"That's my girl."

Yona grunted. "No, no. Just because I agree to talk with you doesn't mean I'm endorsing everything you do. I don't know what you do or who you work for. And I don't think we can have a decent conversation if I'm all tied up like this."

Reuel smiled. Motioned for his assistants take care of Yona. "Bring her all cleaned up to the car. We're going for a ride."

CHAPTER ELEVEN

Kelvin couldn't see anything with a black hood over his head. His hands were still tied behind his back. Two people—one on each side of him—led him on a walk longer than a gangplank on a pirate's ship.

He heard many doors open and shut. The way some of them echoed told him that they were huge doors. Was he back at the hangar? Or was this a warehouse of some sort attached to the hangar?

Finally, they pulled the hood off his head. The room was dark, but right in front of him was a shipping container.

They shoved him into the container and slammed the door behind him.

Kelvin dropped to his knees. Never had he felt

so disappointed with himself. He could go through the entire spectrum of "should not" and he would hit every single one of them.

"Forgive me, Lord!" He fell over into a fetal position and wept.

He tapped the floor. It sounded almost solid. He knew that beneath it was concrete. No escape that way.

Above his head, a small lightbulb hung, caged in an aluminum housing—probably to prevent him from hurting himself.

You think?

Kelvin didn't know whether to laugh or cry— but in this case, he did neither. He was doomed to die, but his only regret was that he had dragged Yona into the pit with him.

"Lord, please keep Yona safe, wherever they've taken her."

And yet...

Yet, Kelvin wasn't overly worried about Yona. She seemed to know Reuel and had some history with him.

Kelvin had no idea who Reuel was. Or Issachar, for that matter.

He prayed that Reuel needed them both alive for whatever reason. Maybe long enough for Dario and Dmitri to mount a rescue.

If they would come at all.

Truly, only God could rescue them now.

It was pointless for Kelvin to pray for absolution. He had taken the ten million dollars. He had worked on MedusaNet, even when warning signs were everywhere.

Kelvin sighed.

Everyone wanted something but no one was satisfied.

Reuel wanted something—whatever it was.

Leland, and therefore Binary Systems, wanted their good reputation restored.

Dario would want to take Kelvin home to the United States for trial—if Yona didn't have first dibs on a trial in Israel for the murder of one Issachar, whom Kelvin didn't even know.

Aspasia was probably still looking for Ulysses. Was he even alive?

And Kelvin? He wanted a chance with Yona, but it was too late now. If she were to count reputation points, he had zero. Or negative.

At the end of the day, all Kelvin had was God.

God—who knew that Kelvin was a sinner and still loved him anyway.

God—who had not forsaken him in spite of his wayward life.

Am I even saved?

Wasn't it true that if he were saved, he wouldn't have sinned so much? So terribly? Causing so much grief with his friends and co-workers?

Kelvin tried to recall a verse he had learned in Sunday school back when he was still attending church. He had memorized I John 1:8-9 because everyone else in class did. Little did he know how true it was of his own life.

> *If we say that we have no sin, we deceive*
> *ourselves, and the truth is not in us. If*
> *we confess our sins, He is faithful and*
> *just to forgive us our sins and to cleanse*
> *us from all unrighteousness.*

"I am sorry, Lord Jesus, for all my sins. I have no excuse."

Kelvin wept.

~

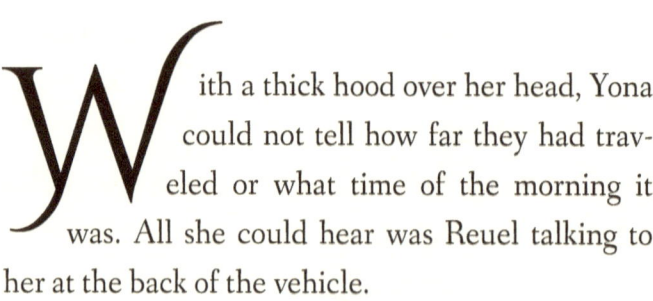

With a thick hood over her head, Yona could not tell how far they had traveled or what time of the morning it was. All she could hear was Reuel talking to her at the back of the vehicle.

From the sometimes-bumpy road beneath, Yona guessed they were still in the countryside somewhere. Probably still in the Czech Republic.

She listened to Reuel drone on, trying to read between the lines, picking apart his sentences. She'd put the reasons together later.

For now, her best bet for staying alive was to let Reuel talk.

Yona filtered out every single reference Reuel quoted from the Bible. She had no confidence in his genuine religiosity, considering what he had done to her and Kelvin. Not only had Reuel broken the law of every nation concerning abduction, he had also sinned against God for lying and misleading Yona into believing that her last job on earth was to assassinate Kelvin.

Now she wanted to live.

And bring Reuel and Ulysses to justice.

She began to realize now that Kelvin was a scapegoat. True, he had worked for the wrong people and gotten paid for it. He was going to get jail time for aiding and abetting terrorists. His reprieve was that he had tried to fix it once he found out who paid his bills.

He had tried to redeem himself.

Only God can redeem us.

Yona tried to pay attention to Reuel, but her

eyes were sleepy. Under the black hood, it felt like nighttime. She could fall asleep right now. However, she had to stay awake to listen to what Reuel had to say.

Something about compensation?

Her wrists hurt from the tight cable ties. "Can you loosen the plastic just a little? I think the circulation in my wrists is getting cut off."

Reuel didn't answer her request. He continued chattering away about something.

Yona lost track of the lecture just as the Royce stopped on some gravel road. She could hear the loud gravel crushed by the tires.

"We're here," Reuel said.

"Where?"

Once again, he ignored Yona. "He'll be so pleased to see you."

"Who?"

No answer.

Her door opened.

"Get out." Someone grabbed her arm.

Slowly, Yona stepped out of the vehicle and followed the lead. There was no way to see through the thick black hood. The fabric was too dense, too tightly-woven.

Her shoes crunched gravel. Yona suspected

they were walking on some driveway where they could park the vehicle.

"Steps," Reuel warned her.

Yona lifted her foot slowly to feel what she was stepping on. She took another step.

She heard a giant door open. It sounded heavy.

Her handler led her in. She almost tripped over what felt like a raised threshold.

She heard the door shut behind her.

All was quiet. No footfalls. No one spoke.

Then someone lifted off her hood. Yona blinked a couple of times to adjust to the light.

When she opened her eyes again, there he was.

The once-dead.

CHAPTER TWELVE

Yona's knees went weak. To think that she had prepared to kill Kelvin Gallagher for being instrumental in the death of her mentor—

Standing right here in front of her in flesh and blood.

He looked a bit older. His face was covered with a heavy beard and mustache. However, Yona recognized the old scar on his left eyebrow and the row of crowded teeth when he smiled.

"Issachar?" Yona barely got the name out. "You're still alive."

Who was buried in his grave in his hometown of Haifa back in Israel? He had wanted to face the top of Mount Carmel and all that.

Suddenly the quick cremation without any autopsy made sense.

"What about your children?" Yona asked. "What are they going to say if they find out they're grieving for nothing?"

"Not for nothing," Issachar answered. "They have my life insurance. They can go on. They'll be fine."

"And you? Are you fine?" Yona's voice cracked.

"I will be when we get our billion dollars."

"We?" Yona glanced at Reuel.

Issachar laughed. "You think Reuel and I had a falling-out? He's still my best buddy. We're doing this for our families."

Families?

Yona's eyes stung.

Issachar's sons were about Yona's age. Would they be happy that their father was still alive so soon after they buried him in their family mausoleum?

"Like what families?" Yona needed clarification.

The events of the last two days had been nothing but bizarre.

"My girlfriend," Issachar replied. "We're going to have kids soon."

Yona's eyes widened. She was sure now that his

grown children would be devastated, not to mention his wife back in Israel, who was still wearing all black.

"You don't believe that an eighty-year-old man can have children?"

He seemed to have forgotten about his family in Israel.

"Genetics is not my field." Yona defended herself.

"Technology these days..." Issachar waved his hands about.

Yep. This was Issachar.

Reuel chuckled.

Strange twinning, these two. One called himself a Christian and the other an atheist. They had banded together like blood brothers before, but this time it was different. This time they seemed to be caught up in something more sinister.

"What are you two up to?" Yona asked. "Is Ulysses involved in this?"

Reuel and Issachar looked at each other.

"Do we care about Ulysses?" Reuel asked.

"Only about his computer system," Issachar replied.

"What do you mean?" Yona tried to put two and two together.

"With the help of overpriced computer consultants, such as Kelvin, Ulysses has rebuilt Medu-saNet to be world class." Issachar walked about. "Unfortunately, he's not sharing the system."

"You're going to make him share."

"Not really." Reuel motioned for Yona's guards to escort her.

She limped, slowing the procession.

They walked down the hallway to what looked like an operations center. There, on a screen nearest Yona, she saw the rooms in the last CIA safe house.

There seemed to be a camera in every room.

The CIA has been compromised.

Reuel led Yona past the row of monitors to a wall of more screens. He showed her several screens and one of them had a man on it, eating lunch. "Did you know that Ulysses wears a wig?"

"Is that real time?" Yona asked.

Reuel nodded.

"Is this room a replica of that one?"

"Yes. We will take over MedusaNet from here," Issachar replied.

"But you're not a computer specialist," Yona said. "And neither is Reuel."

"Not to worry. We hire hackers and computer people to do our bidding."

Yona could guess what would happen to those

hired hands once they were not needed anymore. The same thing that happened to Binary Systems employees—except for Cayson Yang and Kelvin Gallagher, probably.

"Where is Ulysses now?" she asked.

"A chateau outside France."

"You don't have a problem telling me that. Why?" Yona glanced at the other surrounding screens. They showed various parts of the chateau. Mostly empty rooms.

Why couldn't Aspasia find Ulysses when Reuel and Issachar could?

"You're going to help us hack into Ulysses's inner sanctum." Reuel pointed to another screen.

The scene looked like an operations center, like this one she was standing in. Yona looked around her, and then back at the screen.

She leaned against a table to give relief to her ankle. "I'm not a hacker."

"Kelvin is." Issachar pointed to Reuel. "I bet him that Kelvin will do anything for you."

"Me?" Yona laughed.

"You didn't know, I guess, that Kelvin was interested in you when you were observing some of his colleagues in Project Pericarp."

"He invited me to coffee. I said no."

"Because you were in a relationship at that time," Reuel reminded her. "Since your ex-boyfriend is no longer in the picture, you're single and free."

"I'm not for sale." Yona blurted.

"You don't have to do anything, really." Issachar laughed. "Kelvin will bend over backwards if he thinks any harm will come to you. Trust me on that."

"Of course, brother." Reuel shook hands with Issachar. "Anything for the cause."

"What cause?" Yona asked.

"Shall we tell her?" Issachar asked.

"She won't live long to tell others, you mean?" Reuel rubbed his chin.

Yona blinked.

I'm dreaming. Wake up, wake up.

Something was wrong with the conversation, but Yona couldn't pin it down.

"Our cause is to make MedusaNet available to all organizations," Issachar said.

"Let me guess. You don't mean run-of-the-mill organizations."

"Aren't we altruistic, you might wonder?" Reuel seemed disappointed that Yona wasn't happier.

"I trusted the two of you like my own father—

you're like the father I lost." Yona tried to keep her emotions in check.

When her parents had died in some roadside bombing that took out the bus they were riding on, Issachar had been kind to Yona, supporting her through university, reminding her that her father would have done the same thing for Issachar's children.

Issachar had encouraged Yona to serve her country beyond the mandatory military enlistment. He ended up recruiting her for the Mossad.

Just like he had recruited Yona's father when the latter had been in university.

"You look disappointed," Issachar said. "I won't ask you what it's about, but disappointments are a part of life—"

Yona's palm went up to stop him. "Just don't. I don't want to hear any more of your advice."

Reuel opened his mouth to speak.

"You too." Yona pointed her finger at him. "You ply me with Bible verses, making yourself sound like you're a holy man of God. How does what you're doing now square with being a Christian?"

"Fair question." Issachar curled his lips and nodded.

"Well, I think I've fallen away from the faith." Reuel shrugged.

"Or perhaps you never had faith in Jesus Christ in the first place?" Yona asked.

II Timothy 3:4-5 came to her mind.

...traitors, headstrong, haughty, lovers of pleasure rather than lovers of God, having a form of godliness but denying its power. And from such people turn away!

"Maybe you're Judas," Yona added.

"That has a nice ring to it." Issachar laughed.

"Maybe so." Reuel looked more serious. "But do we care, really?"

"God cares."

Reuel laughed. "That's where we part ways, Yona."

"You've been your own god this entire time, using bits and pieces of the Bible to back youself up." Yona's voice broke.

Issachar moved toward the door. "You two can talk all you want, but I'm going to lunch."

Reuel ordered his guards to take Yona away.

"Wait. Aren't you going to invite me to lunch?" Yona asked. Three could play crazy. "For old times' sake?"

"No!" They both said at once.

Yona wanted them to keep talking, but that

would have to wait. If they talked and told her enough, she could bring all that evidence home to Mossad—

Oh wait.

I quit.

She felt alone. So alone.

CHAPTER THIRTEEN

Kelvin hadn't seen Yona in the last twenty-four hours, and he was beginning to worry. No, freak out. No, worry. Probably both.

The last time he had seen her, they were both tied up on some warehouse floor. Their enemy had taken him away and put him in a shipping container. He had fallen asleep for who knew how long.

They woke him up sometime later, and drove him around with a hood over his head. He had fallen asleep again in the vehicle.

And had woken up in this dungeon. For the most part, it was a dry basement of some sort, with stone walls all around. The ceiling lights shone on rows of computer workstations, but he was the only one deposited in this room.

There was a small bathroom—a toilet and sink —on one end. He washed his face in the sink. No paper towels. He let his face air dry because his shirt was too dirty to be used to wipe his face.

For a man who was probably going to die, he hadn't lost his sense of hygiene.

He found a comfortable chair to sit in. They were all alike, but this one didn't squeak. Also, it was in front of the largest screen in the room.

He figured if he was dropped off here, they— whoever they were—would want him to work, and he'd take the biggest screen, thank you.

As he waited, his thoughts kept turning back to Yona. And the more he thought of her, the more anxious he became.

He closed his eyes to recall some scripture he had studied in his scattered past. A long time ago, Cayson invited him to church at Midtown Chapel. Kelvin went because he had been saved as a teenager, although he hadn't been serious about it.

In the several years he had worked for Binary Systems, he attended sporadic church services with Cayson. His faith wasn't as strong as Cayson's either.

And then Mother's cancer came and ruined his life.

Well, in retrospect, he had forgotten God. He had gone his own way.

"Am I a prodigal son, Lord?" Kelvin mumbled. "I want to come back to You, Lord. Please forgive me, and take me back."

His words echoed in the silent room.

"It's my fault that Yona is in trouble. It will be ugly if they use her against me," Kelvin whispered to himself.

He felt a headache coming. It usually came when he felt stressed. "Yes, I'm worried."

Philippians 4:6 reminded him not to be anxious, but to pray and trust God.

Be anxious for nothing, but in everything by prayer and supplication, with thanksgiving, let your requests be made known to God;

Kelvin felt like he was bursting with worry for Yona. And she probably had no idea he had any thought of her. She probably thought all he ever considered was his own selfish self.

Well, it would have been true four years before, or three, or even perhaps the year before.

But not now.

Sitting here in the underground catacombs of what looked like an old castle—his tomb, his doom —Kelvin decided he could not think merely of himself anymore. If anything, his prayer was for God to free Yona.

She didn't deserve the punishment.

This was his fault, not hers.

His own doing.

He had no one else to blame but himself.

Before he could continue his confession to God, the door opened to a rumble of noises and voices.

All three prisoners had hoods over their heads. Surrounding them were the same armed men who had hauled Kelvin into this room hours before.

"Please! Please!" A woman's voice from under one of those black hoods.

It didn't sound like Yona's, but it was familiar to Kelvin. She sounded like...

One of the men lifted the hood off her.

"Danika?" Kelvin couldn't believe his eyes. "Danika Svoboda?"

"Kelvin!" Danika rushed forward, but the men held her back. "I thought you were dead!"

"I thought you were dead too." Kelvin waited for the other hoods to come off.

And he would've fallen off the chair had he still been sitting.

Vivek Rao in flesh and blood.

Vivek, who was supposed to be dead in the USA over a year prior.

Were these clones? The thought ran through Kelvin's mind, though he knew that could not be true—not in this day and age.

Vivek yelled when he saw Kelvin and started charging at him, even though his wrists were tied up. "You! This is all your fault!"

The men held him back. Muttered to one another—something about needing to babysit the hackers.

"I'm sorry," Kelvin said. Whatever it was, he was sure Vivek was right. "It's my fault."

He wondered how Vivek and Danika were still alive, considering the DNA results...

Ah, the DNA results could have been fabricated by interfering with the computers they were stored in.

Who'd do that though?

He could only think of one person.

Ulysses.

As soon as the men released Danika from her bonds, she pressed her fingers on Vivek's arm. "I'm not dreaming."

"Neither am I." Vivek looked at Danika a certain way.

"That can wait, lovebirds," Kelvin said. "Where's Jamal?"

Nobody could answer him.

Maybe Jamal wasn't dead either. Cayson would be happy to hear that. In fact, he'd be happy to hear that most of his team wasn't dead.

"What do they want from us?" Danika looked at Kelvin, as if he'd know.

He shrugged. "We're all waiting to find out."

All the screens flickered on at once. A wall-mounted screen came to life.

Reuel appeared on the screen. "To answer your question, Kelvin, your assignment is to hijack MedusaNet."

"MedusaNet? It was destroyed last year," Kelvin reminded his captor.

"Nope. On the contrary, Ulysses is trying to rebuild it. You're going to take it away from him."

"For what compensation?" Vivek asked.

"Your life. You capture MedusaNet, we release you." Reuel said it as if he meant it.

That was when Kelvin decided that Reuel couldn't possibly be telling the truth. If they wanted to live, they had to find a way out themselves. But not without Yona.

"Where is Yona?" Kelvin asked.

"Our insurance is right here." Reuel motioned to someone off-screen.

Yona was pushed into the camera view. She looked a bit disheveled.

She gasped. "Whoa. Is anyone else not dead?"

CHAPTER FOURTEEN

The problem with the members of a team knowing they were going to die, was that it killed their motivation. Nothing Kelvin said—whether explicitly or implicitly—could make Vivek and Danika do what Reuel wanted: take over the new MedusaNet from Ulysses.

Kelvin found himself working hard alone, surrounded by Vivek and Danika squabbling with each other in their last days on earth.

As soon as Reuel appeared on the screen again, Kelvin threw up his hands. "Kill us already!"

The door clicked open.

"What did you ask them to do to us?" Danika screamed at Kelvin.

The men came in, and without a word, they cuffed Vivek and dragged him out.

Danika pounded on the door. "You can't do this to us! We're human beings too!"

Onscreen, Reuel cleared his throat. "From your conversation with each other, I realized that you need an incentive to get this project completed."

Kelvin glanced at Danika. *What have you done?*

"We're holding Vivek and Yona until we have control of MedusaNet," Reuel said.

Kelvin raised his hand.

"What, Kelvin?" Reuel frowned.

"It's not called MedusaNet anymore. Ulysses renamed it Telemachus."

"Son of a...hmm... Not unexpected."

Kelvin had no opinion. If Ulysses—real name unknown—wanted to name it after his mythological son, Telemachus, who was he to object? However, to keep it all Greek, Ulysses should have called himself Odysseus, rather than the Latinized version of his name.

Then again, what did Kelvin care? He was stuck in here without a bargaining chip, imprisoned with a screaming woman gone berserk who might not be able to do the job without her beau.

However, since he had nothing to lose...

"Reuel, three meals a day together with our

friends, daily showers, and clean clothes. Is that too much to ask?" Kelvin went for it.

"No sleep? You're not asking for beds?"

"Considering you seem to be in a hurry to take over MedusaNet—Telemachus—I wouldn't think we'd get much sleep." Kelvin paused, as if thinking, which he really was. He pointed to an empty corner by the wall. "However, since you mentioned it, a couple of cots over there might be a gesture of kindness and good faith."

Reuel laughed. "I can see why Aspasia kept you alive. You don't take sides, do you?"

Kelvin used to take the side of money, but now that he was older, money had no hold on him as much as people did.

And God.

He had repented.

Yet, he was still in this hole in the ground that he had to crawl out of. Galatians 6:7 came to his mind in a flash.

> Do not be deceived, God is not mocked; for whatever a man sows, that he will also reap.

Kelvin knew he was reaping the sin he had sown. His soul was forgiven, but that didn't remove the consequences of his sin.

This could be his death sentence, though he would go to Heaven with a free conscience.

"Please?" Kelvin asked.

"You're asking for a lot. Three meals a day, showers, clothes, and two cots."

"Do you want Telemachus or not?" Kelvin kept his voice even, although his heart was beating fast.

Reuel paused. And then he nodded.

An hour later, one cot appeared in the corner. Kelvin and Danika had to hot bunk when they took turns napping.

Kelvin checked on Danika from time to time. "You okay?"

Danika was still crying. Her mascara ran down her cheeks, making her look like some punk rock star. Her purple hair—with her blonde roots showing—didn't help. She looked a mess.

Several hours later, Kelvin and Danika were taken separately to a shower. The water was slow and cold, but Kelvin didn't care. They had given him a bar of soap, and he almost used it up, scrubbing gunk off his scalp and skin.

Feeling clean, Kelvin waited for Danika. She also looked better after her shower. In fact, her face looked brighter.

Kelvin prayed for Danika. He wasn't sure if she was saved, but the main thing right now was for

God to keep her calm. If she could stop screaming, they might make better progress in their work for Reuel.

Armed guards came to usher them to a room with no chairs or tables. On the floor was a large plastic sheet. And paper plates of food.

"Where do we wash our hands?" Kelvin asked.

Danika laughed so hard it echoed in the room. Then she slapped him on his arm. "You're always the optimist among us."

Kelvin had never looked at himself as an optimist. In fact, he still felt that he was the prodigal son.

I want to go home, Lord. Please take me back.

He knew God had forgiven him, but he didn't feel it. His situation currently didn't help.

When the door opened again, and Yona walked in, Kelvin nearly cried.

S tale bread, old apples, questionable water.
That was their lunch, but Yona was simply happy to have some food and to be with Kelvin—

Wait. What?

She knew that whatever they said would be recorded for Reuel and Issachar.

Yes, Issachar.

Her once-mentor, now an enemy of the state of Israel.

God will judge him.

How could she speak in cryptic messages to Kelvin? How could she tell him that Issachar was part of the setup? That the entire situation was bigger than them?

Then again, was that important?

It was all in the past. All done. All over.

If she only had five minutes to spare with Kelvin, she had to make every minute count. There was no guarantee Reuel would let them eat lunch together tomorrow.

She felt uncomfortable when Vivek and Danika kissed in front of her. It wasn't like she hadn't seen anyone kiss before, but they were in prison!

When she looked back at the apple core in her hand, she felt someone touch her arm.

"How's your ankle?" Kelvin asked quietly.

"Better. I get to rest a lot, so no pressure on it."

"Good. Are they treating you well?"

"For a prisoner, I guess. Reuel told me you

asked for a picnic." Reuel had also told her more, but Yona didn't need to get into all that right now.

Kelvin seemed genuinely happy to see her, and she didn't want to spoil his joy by telling him that she knew he had been interested in her for a while now.

To be fair, she hadn't given Kelvin much thought until Reuel fed her erroneous intel about Issachar's non-murderer.

"Not exactly a picnic. I asked for three meals a day. I guess he didn't want Danika and Vivek to hurt each other if we had tables and chairs."

"Yeah?" Yona chuckled. "They don't look like they're fighting at this moment."

Vivek and Danika weren't shy about their public display of affection.

Kelvin drew a deep breath. "I'm sorry, Yona."

"We all are."

"I'll make up for it," he whispered in her ear.

Yona didn't push him back because she realized this was how they could communicate. She leaned in toward his ear. "Homing beacon."

It was all she said.

Kelvin ran a thumb across her chin and smiled. He planted a kiss on her cheek.

"Brilliant," he whispered.

CHAPTER FIFTEEN

A call to action. A directive. A suggestion.
Call it whatever, but Kelvin had his
marching orders now.

For the next several days and nights, as he and
Danika hacked into Telemachus to gain control of
the VPN for Reuel, he looked for ways to plant a
homing beacon that would contact Leland Yang-
Joule, the only person Kelvin knew who might be
able to read it as a call for help.

Might.

Nothing was a sure thing.

Kelvin wished he could have more hands on
deck. He voiced the concern to Reuel the next time
he appeared onscreen.

"You realize that Vivek is part of my team," Kelvin reminded him. "Yona is neither a hacker nor a systems specialist."

The elderly man made a face, and the screen cleared.

Sometime later, Vivek returned to the computer room, accompanied by a guard.

Kelvin wondered why the guard didn't leave.

Whenever Danika scooted her chair over to Vivek's workstation, the guard made some sort of low-level grunting noise. It sounded like *grrr* or something.

Kelvin couldn't help chuckling.

Reuel had sent a watchdog.

"How far along are we?" Vivek asked.

Kelvin spun around in his chair. "DMZ. Glad you're here. We should be able to get in soon."

"Nice to be needed." Vivek nodded. "Hey, thanks for asking for the meals. I think I'm gaining all the weight I lost in the last few months."

Kelvin didn't want to ask more, but he figured they ran too. Perhaps they had it better than he did because they ran together.

Kelvin had been alone in that abandoned building.

Well, not entirely alone.

He had Mordecai the stray cat.

And God.

Most of all, he had God.

God never left him nor forsook him.

Thank You, Jesus. Help me succeed, please.

T
hey spent the next few days chipping away at the security system around Telemachus. It was military grade, but nothing Binary Systems hackers couldn't handle.

Ulysses must not have had proper help because at the core of Telemachus was the network structure that Binary Systems had put in place several years prior. Kelvin and Cayson had designed it.

If he planted the homing beacon at the right places, whenever the VPN was activated, it would send signals to several sites around the world that Kelvin knew Leland and Cayson would check. If their tools could triangulate where the signals originated, they could send someone—Dario, maybe—to rescue them.

Endless hours later, they were inside Telemachus, wandering around, checking on failsafe measures that Ulysses had hacked together. It was messy, but it wasn't his system.

"Are you ready for root?" Kelvin asked Vivek.

In a corner, Danika was asleep. She hadn't slept in about three days. Her mouth hung open and she had been out for hours.

Vivek nodded. "Too bad there's nothing in this for us."

"Maybe the satisfaction that we hacked into the system in five days?"

"No glory in that, dude. We're all going to die."

Kelvin actually smiled. "I don't fear death. I'm going to Heaven."

"How can you even know that to be a fact?"

"The Bible says so."

Vivek shook his head. "And you believe it. No questions asked? Blind faith and all that?"

"It's not blind faith. I know whom I believe." Kelvin wasn't sure how else to explain his faith. He knew in his heart that he was a believer in Jesus. That was all he knew.

"Whatever floats your boat, man."

Kelvin said no more.

They worked in tandem to hack into the root account. If Kelvin didn't know any better, he would say that Ulysses had left a back door for him. Left the lights on.

One could say that it was as easy as walking in through an open front door.

However, because of that, Kelvin wondered if this was a trap.

Who was Ulysses trying to catch?

CHAPTER SIXTEEN

One benefit of knowing more than his employer—or in this case, captors—was the freedom to add or subtract functionality to the computer system at will without their knowledge.

To Kelvin's delight, the kill switch he had implanted into the old MedusaNet had carried over to Telemachus in a fractured sense—part of the code was still functional.

He could see the pieces that he had debugged and fixed—the last thing he had done before Aspasia lost him to the FSB, just moments before he activated it.

From what Leland had told him in the van the week before—had it been a week?—the kill switch was in Cayson's head, but who had put it there? Was it Neon before he died? Or was it someone else?

"Kel, I'm done debugging," Vivek called out from his corner of the room. "You can test run it, if you want, but I think it's green for go."

Vivek lumbered toward the cot and dropped onto it. Within seconds, he began to snore.

Danika was asleep at her keyboard, head in her folded arms on the table.

The wall-mounted screen came to life.

"You done?" Reuel asked.

Sitting next to him was someone Kelvin had not seen before.

"Do you have the admin account?" he asked.

He had heard that voice before. Some time ago. And that accent. Was he Israeli, by any chance?

Could he be...

Could he be Neon's handler?

It was a shot in the dark. Kelvin decided the probability for that to happen was very low.

"Yes, we just reached *root*." Actually, it was almost two hours before, but he needed that much time to activate what he had left unfinished the last time he was inside MedusaNet.

Kelvin couldn't recall why he didn't have enough time to finish the second malware he added to the system the year before. He wondered sometimes if he was slowing down.

At thirty-three years old?

He wasn't sure if age had anything to do with it. He yawned.

Or a lack of sleep.

After this, he decided he would sleep for days. Maybe weeks.

Well, he might get his wish. There would be plenty of time to sleep in jail.

"Do we have control of Telemachus?" Reuel asked.

Kelvin nodded. "If you heard Vivek, he just finished debugging some procedures. I need to run some final tests, and then it's all yours."

"Very good. No more lunches with your sweethearts until this process is complete," Reuel said.

"To be sure, Ulysses is going to know as soon as we cut off control to the VPN," Kelvin warned him. "Are you prepared for that?"

"We have his location surrounded," the other man said. "Don't worry about Ulysses."

"I'm sorry, I didn't catch your name." Kelvin felt braver now that he had the upper hand in the transaction.

"It's not your concern. Get us Telemachus."

"And we go free? All four of us?"

"That's the agreement."

But it might not be the plan. Kelvin was sure now that he had to find a way out. The homing beacon had to work.

As soon as he made the switch and kicked Ulysses's system administrators off the VPN, the homing beacon would transmit the location of their new machine room.

If it worked.

Please, Lord, let it work.

Danika stirred from her table. "Are we ready to test?"

"Yes." Kelvin looked up at the camera mounted on top of the wall screen. "If you'd excuse us, we have work to do. I will let you know as soon as we're done."

Danika typed furiously on the keyboard.

Vivek snored on the cot.

Kelvin prayed his old software pieces he had completed tonight—or was it day?—would not fail him now. He ran the malware in the background. If it worked, it would completely obliterate Telemachus once and for all.

"What's that..." Danika sounded perplexed.

"Diagnostics. Ulysses has a habit of adding background processes that might prevent us from doing a complete takeover. We need to eliminate all those before we proceed, obviously."

"Okay." She still looked a bit confused.

"Why don't you wake up, Vivek? We need all hands on deck." Kelvin hoped his voice didn't sound nervous.

As soon as Danika stepped away from her workstation, Kelvin activated the homing beacon.

One shot.

That was all he had.

If it failed, all of their lives would be in the hands of Reuel and his co-conspirator.

If it succeeded, Leland would get someone to come over here to rescue them. Perhaps Dario and the CIA. Perhaps INTERPOL. He didn't care who, as long as they were rescuers.

Kelvin knew that he would be arrested, tried for treason, and incarcerated.

He prayed that the sentence would be swift.

He wasn't sure how long it was going to be. Perhaps the judge and jury would see that he had tried his best to correct the error of his ways.

When he had found out what Aspasia wanted him to do, he had installed a kill switch that brought down the old MedusaNet.

Now he was activating not only a homing beacon so the calvary could find them, but also installing a malware that would destroy any failsafe measures in the new Telemachus VPN.

Thank God this wasn't more than a virtual private network.

Perhaps all these good deeds he had done or was doing would help him get a lighter sentence. However, if they did not, Kelvin was prepared to accept whatever came his way.

If he had to go to prison for many years, then that was what he deserved.

His only regret would be losing Yona.

God would still be with him in prison, but would Yona wait for a convict?

Why would she?

CHAPTER SEVENTEEN

At lunch the next day, Kelvin whispered to Yona that the peanut butter and jelly sandwich almost tasted homemade.

Yona had no idea what he was referring to, and there was no way to ask him to explain without listening ears and prying eyes on the ceiling and all around them.

He mentioned *home* a few more times.

Oh.

Maybe he was referring to the homing beacon.

Danika started to cry and Vivek comforted her.

Yona prayed for them silently. At some point, people could break under a tremendous amount of stress, especially if they hadn't slept much all week.

"Maybe they'll let you rest for a few days," Yona said. "What's next?"

"Whatever they want us to do, I guess," Kelvin said.

"I'm surprised that Ulysses broke so easily." Yona ate the little breadcrumbs left on her paper plate. The bread was stale, but food was food. There was probably too much sugar in the jam.

"It's only been about eighteen hours," Vivek said.

"That's an eternity on the internet." Yona drank some water.

"Maybe, but considering Ulysses is not a techie, maybe they have no idea their network has been compromised."

"True, Viv." Kelvin folded up his paper plate into a half-moon shape.

Yona didn't know why he did that. Something to do, perhaps.

Lunch was over and they were separated again after the guards tied up their wrists. Yona nodded to the trio and headed in another direction from them, back to her room upstairs, which she called her holding pen.

Every now and then, after lunch, Reuel talked with her, as if that would absolve him of his sins. It did nothing for Yona. She couldn't even pray for him.

Reuel had betrayed her trust.

More importantly, he had used Bible passages to gain Yona's trust. He knew that Yona was a Christian who believed that Jesus Christ was the Messiah of the world. The Savior. The Redeemer. The Lord of all.

And he had exploited her belief and shaken her faith.

Perhaps it was a good thing.

I don't know.

Walking on both sides of her were her two usual guards. They would remove her ties before they locked her in her pen. She had thought of fighting back, but the two men were like Goliaths to her David-sized self.

She didn't have five river stones.

Walking along the upstairs hallway, Yona heard the noise of people fighting in a room with its door ajar.

What on earth?

At first the guards ignored the commotion.

Yona heard voices. Reuel and Issachar were yelling at each other.

Then Yona heard a shot. And another.

Weapon raised, one of the guards let go of

Yona's arm and rushed to the room. The other guard held Yona back.

The door opened.

On the floor inside the room, someone was sprawled on the floor.

Standing over him, Reuel put away his pistol. "Now I get a hundred percent."

Yona lunged forward, pulling the guard with her.

As she got closer to the door, she saw the face of the man on the floor. A growing pool of blood spread on the floor beneath his torso.

"Issachar!" Yona choked out the word.

"Shut the door!" Reuel waved frantically.

A guard slammed the door in Yona's face.

The guard took her back to her room, leaving her alone to weep.

CHAPTER EIGHTEEN

"Truth be told, he was already dead to his family, and at one point, to you as well." Reuel sat on a chair that his guard had brought into the holding pen.

Yona sat on her small bed, her back against the wall, and her chin on her folded knee. She didn't know how to respond to Reuel, who had felt the need to explain away what he had done.

It might look weird for her to converse with a murderer. However, there was no one else to talk to the rest of the day—not until dinnertime, anyway.

Besides, if she could gain Reuel's trust—in their new non-relationship—perhaps she could find a way to defeat him.

Maybe.

Maybe not.

Still, she was willing to give it a shot—uh, try.

"I know you don't care what I have to say, but Issachar and I had a fight, and I won." Somehow Reuel must have felt a need to explain his actions.

"Must everything be about you winning?" Yona sighed. Ever since she had known Reuel, he had always been competitive. But must every competition end in the death of his opponents? "I thought Issachar was your friend, or at least a business partner."

"He outlived his usefulness."

"As will I." The solemn realization hit Yona harder than she expected.

"Yes, but I need you alive. Issachar—well, he was redundant, to be honest with you."

"What was that about anyway? What couldn't you resolve with a discussion rather than death?" Yona wiped tears on her sleeves.

She didn't know why she grieved so much a second time. Together with Issachar's family, she had come to the point of accepting that he had died, only to find him very much alive in the Czech Republic, and trying to become the next terrorist leader after Molyneux.

"He wanted fifty-one percent of Telemachus."

"What's one percent?"

"It cost him his life, didn't it?"

Yona sniffed. "How about living to fight another day?"

"You think I'd be compassionate toward him tomorrow? He wants another one percent. That essentially means I will lose one percent. Do you know what one percent of a hundred million dollars is?"

"Is Telemachus worth that much?"

"And more."

"Are you hoping to replace Molyneux?" Yona thought that Ulysses wanted that position.

"I already have."

"It's greed, isn't it? You want to rule the world, and you don't want to share the throne with Issachar."

"I'm already sitting on the throne." Reuel stroked his trimmed beard.

"So you have Telemachus all to yourself. Happy now?"

"Very much so." Reuel slapped his own thighs. "It's a happy day today."

"At the expense of someone else's life."

"We make sacrifices."

"As long as the sacrifice is not yours?" Yona could see that if she continued that way, jabbing at his conscience, he might snap. She needed to calm him down. "So Issachar was your sacrifice at the altar of power."

"That might have been his reason for existence."

"May I see his body?"

"It's being disposed of."

"What if that wasn't him on the floor?"

"It was. Trust me."

Yona stretched out her legs on the thin mattress. Her ankle didn't hurt anymore. "People have 'died' and then come back to life. Vivek and Danika for example. How?"

"We hid them—Issachar and I. Hacked into the DNA labs and changed the data to match the dead stand-ins."

"Who hacked?" Yona hoped it wasn't Kelvin.

"Well, we have people."

"Are they still around?"

No reply.

"Maybe stashed away for another day."

"Maybe."

"So how do we know you aren't hiding Issachar somewhere?"

Reuel laughed. "You know me better than that. Does a throne have two kings?"

"Does a serpent have two heads?"

"I don't even know what that means."

"I don't either." Yona dared not make eye contact. "You know, I wonder if, in the process of hunting down Israel's enemies, you have now become one."

"Me? Nah. I'm everybody's enemy, not only Israel's. In fact, sometimes I'm my own enemy."

Yona had to agree with him. Estranged from his own wife of fifty years and his three sons, who didn't want to have anything to do with his activities in Europe, Reuel lived a sad and lonely life indeed, isolated from his family and friends.

Yona wondered if he could have found happiness had he been truly saved. All those Bible verses Reuel had recited had probably been to gain her trust. Why take the trouble? He could have applied those Bible verses to himself, his own life.

Jesus could forgive him of his sins. "There's forgiveness in Jesus Christ."

Reuel got up from his chair. They were still alone in the room. His guards were outside. "That's for you, not for me. I'm outside the reach of God."

Yona felt sorry for Reuel. He wasn't a real believer in Christ after all. And yet... "No one is beyond the reach of God."

Reuel stopped at the door. "Then let me ask you a question. Why didn't God stop me before I shot Issachar?"

"You were filled with rage all on your own. God didn't plant sin in your heart." Yona felt brave enough to keep talking. "However, Jesus' blood at the cross cleanses us from all sins."

"All your work at Mossad? You killed people too."

"Enemies of Israel."

"There's that word again. What is an enemy, Yona? Pray tell."

Before Yona could speak, Reuel cut her off. "I'll figure out my own way to the other side. You don't have to try to help me at all."

"There's only one path to Heaven and His name is Jesus."

At first Reuel turned quiet. Then he burst into a chortle. "Why, Miss Yona. If I didn't know you any better, I'd say you were trying to preach some Jesus into me."

"Just telling you what I know, is all."

"I have to give it to you. You've always cared for my well-being." Reuel's voice turned pensive. "I came here to do a pulse check on you. I don't want you to be angry with me, but I know you probably are. Issachar was your mentor. For that, I'm sorry."

"That he was my mentor or that you killed him?"

"Maybe a bit of both."

Reuel slowly called her name. "I've always been patient with you. Treated you like my daughter."

"Yet somehow I know you will not let me leave this place." Yona straightened up. "Not me, or Kelvin, or Danika, or Vivek. Am I right?"

"I need a network administration team."

"I'm not in IT. You know that. You also don't trust me enough to put me on your security team. What am I doing here? This is a huge VPN. You're going to need more IT staff than Kelvin and his friends."

Reuel shrugged. "I think they can handle it."

"The VPN is worldwide. It cannot go down ever if you want your clients to call your system reliable."

"I know that, Yona. I know that." He didn't look worried.

"Now that you've eliminated your business partner, how are you going to grow your business alone?" Yona wouldn't use those words to describe a terrorist organization, but she had to find Reuel's soft spot.

"Are you trying to get yourself a job?" Reuel laughed. Then he turned serious. "You're insurance."

"Insurance? When I'm of no use to you anymore, what then? Will you *Issachar* me?"

Reuel laughed. "You know me too well. But I tell you what. If you don't comply, then I'll get rid of your friend downstairs."

"Then you'll have no IT department."

"I'll find people. There will always be people."

"Not as good as them. You have some of the world's top computer specialists working for you for free. It will affect your bottom line if you get rid of them." Yona only said that because she didn't want Reuel to kill them prematurely, not before Kelvin's homing beacon worked.

Yona prayed someone would come to rescue them. Her job now was to buy as much time as possible.

Reuel seemed to study her. "You're a confusing person, you know?"

Yona didn't say anything.

"I saw you and Kelvin every day at lunch. I would assume that you two have a thing for each other." Reuel didn't wait for her to answer. "I don't know how you feel about eliminating Kelvin, but I know he would do anything not to lose you."

"Lose me? We're not an item. There's nothing —no one—to lose."

"Not yet. Just not yet."

CHAPTER NINETEEN

That night, the rain fell hard on the old castle, and Kelvin could hear the thunder from the computer room. He was worried that the electricity would go out and that there would be no uninterruptible power supply. Without UPS and a generator, they might have to stop working altogether.

Sure enough, the power fluctuated several times, accompanied by Danika's screams. Kelvin hadn't pegged her as one who'd be afraid of the dark, but there she was, huddled in a corner screaming murder.

Kelvin asked Reuel for a time-out.

Any delay is a good delay.

It would buy time for his homing beacon to

work.

"I'm surprised you don't have a backup generator," Kelvin said.

Onscreen, Reuel looked like he was about to doze off. Kelvin wondered where the other man had gone, and what his name was. He almost asked, but he didn't let his curiosity get the better of him. Better stay out of politics.

"If we don't shut down the computers in this room, one lightning strike might take them all out," Kelvin warned.

"You're trying to scare us." Reuel pointed a finger at the camera.

"I'm just sharing my own experiences. I worked at a place once that had backups, but their entire building wasn't properly grounded—"

Craaaccckkk!

And the lights went out.

"As I was saying..." Kelvin spoke into the utter darkness, his words pierced by Danika's screams in concert with thunder strikes that seemed to be right above them or on the ground outside their dungeon.

"There is a God," Vivek said.

Yona awoke with a start. Sitting in the dark on her bed, she listened to the heavy rain and thunder. There were no windows in her holding pen, and the walls were stone, but the thunder was so loud she felt like it was just on the other side of the wall.

The ceiling light had gone out.

Whether Yona closed or opened her eyes, it made no difference. The room was completely dark. In these times, her hearing sharpened.

Thunder. Rain. Thunder. Rain—

Footsteps outside her door.

Boots.

Heavy boots.

Then an explosion so bright and loud that Yona covered her eyes and ears.

"Yona Epstein?" A man's voice said.

He had an accent.

Who are they?

She didn't reply.

"Yona?" Louder this time.

"Yes, yes." Yona turned her face away from the flashlight.

"Let's go home!" It was in Hebrew.

"My friends are downstairs," Yona replied.

"Show the way." He motioned for someone to give Yona a vest.

By that gesture, Yona knew who they were. They would never say so in public, but these were the people in the world who would come to her rescue anywhere, no matter what. These were the elite of the elites.

"Thank you."

"You have some explaining to do." Another voice broke through.

Uh-oh. A long-time buddy in the Metsada, Hadassah had partnered with Yona many times. This time, Yona had left her university friend behind. In fact, she had left the entire Mossad behind.

"Deserting us when we need you most." Hadassah shook her head. "What did you have? A lapse of judgment?"

"Nice to see you too." Yona buckled up her vest. "A Beretta for me?"

"No. You don't work for us anymore, remember?"

"Bummer." Yona showed them the stairs. Reluctantly, she let them usher her out of the building.

Rain poured in buckets. Yona could hardly see where she was going. She followed the Mossad agent in front of her, who handed her to another agent. Never once did they turn her over to anyone who wasn't Mossad.

The castle was surrounded by military personnel and their armored vehicles. Here and there, Yona spotted local police vehicles with the word *Policie* emblazoned on the doors and hoods.

Unmarked vehicles of unknown origins filled the rest of the entrance.

Yona stayed a safe distance away, inside a large van to keep out of the rain. No one said anything to her. They knew who she was, and someone motioned for her to sit down in an empty seat, but she preferred to stand.

She monitored the bank of screens they were all looking at. She tried to find one that showed Hadassah and her team.

"Down the hallway," someone said. "At the end of the hallway... There."

Their flashlights shone at once in the dark, making shadows here and there. The door was bolted.

"I think it's six inches thick," Yona told them.

Someone nodded and relayed the information to Hadassah. They set the charges, and brought the wall down in no time.

A piercing scream pushed through the smoke.

"Danika." Yona smiled. She was alive. Maybe the rest might be too.

Hadassah's team brought out Vivek and then Kelvin.

Yona was so relieved to see Kelvin that she had to sit down.

Twenty minutes later, the joint Israel-Czech paramilitary team came out, and the police went in.

Still no sign of Reuel. "Where is Reuel?"

Yona's question went unanswered. The castle was clear. There were dead guards here and there, but no Reuel.

Hadassah entered the van, all wet. "They knew we breached the compound."

"How did they escape so quickly?" As soon as Yona asked, she knew the answer. "Underground tunnels, maybe?"

"We're checking all tunnels. I'll go see what they find." Hadassah exited the van to talk to her counterpart about that.

Yona knew they had a big problem on their hands if Reuel escaped.

The tug-of-war between Reuel and Ulysses over the newly resurrected VPN could spell trouble.

"Ideally the two would duke it out and take out each other," someone in the van said.

Obviously, they had been briefed. "But we don't live in an ideal world. This world is a mess."

They said no more to Yona.

Hadassah returned. "No tunnels. They were all sealed up. Reuel probably left in a vehicle."

"So he knew you were coming." Yona wondered if anyone intercepted the homing beacon. "May I ask how you knew to come get us here?"

"Kelvin's homing beacon reached the CIA. They called us because Reuel is our problem."

"Since when was the CIA ever a hands-off organization?"

Hadassah shrugged. "We got you."

"Where are the others?" Particularly, Yona wanted to see Kelvin.

"The CIA has them."

"All three?"

"All three." Hadassah put up a gloved finger. "Don't go out there. They've left."

Oh.

CHAPTER TWENTY

S tanding trial in a foreign country had crossed Kelvin's mind once or twice after the FSB dropped him off in Prague. Left to die, so to speak. Even Russia didn't want to have anything to do with him anymore.

Dying hadn't been in his time in Prague. He was convinced of that when nobody came to kill him in the months he had been hiding in the abandoned building.

Don't everybody come at once!

Mossad and the CIA came at the same time, along with Aspasia.

Kelvin wondered what Aspasia was doing these days. Had she found Ulysses? Had both of them been arrested?

Kelvin smiled to no one in his jail cell in Prague, awaiting trial for knowingly working for terrorists. Well, he hadn't known it at first, and when he realized who Molyneux was, he had no way to get out of the situation.

The US Embassy had appointed him a bilingual lawyer who could argue his case in court. The lawyer was familiar with some of the projects that CIA informants did in Europe, so he tried to paint Kelvin as someone who worked undercover for the CIA, got caught in a bad deal, and then tried to worm his way out of the mess with various malware, hidden codes, backdoors, and whatever else he could throw at the enemy's network.

It could all work out in the end.

He wondered why the CIA had handed him over to the Prague Police. Perhaps there was political pressure. Perhaps they wanted to protect CIA assets on the ground and in the surrounding countries.

Kelvin knew that his jail time would decrease if he could deliver Aspasia and Ulysses to the International Criminal Court.

However, they might lie, and that wouldn't help.

The proof was in the pudding.

According to his attorney, the CIA and Mossad had taken apart the basement computer room. Kelvin had given them the *root* password so that they could take over the system.

He still didn't believe that Ulysses had given up the network so easily.

Something was amiss.

But he couldn't put his finger on it.

All he could do now was pray that God would help him through this, no matter what he deserved.

I ask that You'll be with me wherever I go, Lord.

Right now, he was stuck here for the fourth week. He had asked for an English Bible, pen, and paper. Most of the time, the pen remained unused and the paper blank.

Throughout the first week, he spent time reading Paul's epistles.

In the second week behind bars, he started reading Genesis. He thought that maybe he could read through the Bible and see how far along in jail he would be when he reached the last chapter of the Book of Revelation.

He might get out of jail sooner if...

A thought crossed his mind.

"Why didn't I think of that sooner?" He started scribbling on the paper they had given him.

When his attorney visited him that afternoon, he handed the paper over to him for delivery.

And he prayed with all his heart that he was right.

CHAPTER TWENTY-ONE

Dmitri walked with a cane that looked like it could be a weapon. Yona didn't want to find out, but he kept brandishing it like a sword. He probably didn't need the cane.

They had just come out of a meeting, and were going into another meeting.

Yona felt like she was being recruited into some clandestine operation beyond what Mossad usually did. She hadn't decided if she would work for Dmitri, but the free flight from Prague to Vienna, a safe place for her to stay and rest, and a high-paying job all enticed her to no end.

"You remind me of someone's daughter," he

had said for the last two weeks since Yona arrived in Vienna.

Yet the elderly gentleman hadn't disclosed who she reminded him of.

The hallway was opulently decorated in an old-world baroque style. The calm colors belied the fact that this was Dmitri's operational center in their mission to destroy all traces of MedusaNet, also known as Telemachus.

"You'd want to know that Kelvin is doing well in prison." Dmitri opened a door that led to another hallway. "His trial is in two days."

Yona noticed that Dmitri was wearing medical gloves. *Not leaving fingerprints?*

"Thank you for the information." Yona was appreciative, but she didn't think it was anyone's business whom she was interested in.

Besides, he could be incarcerated for a very long time.

Nothing would come of it.

"I've sent him my best lawyers," Dmitri added.

"Thank you."

They entered a meeting room. They were alone.

"When he comes out, I want him to work for me in Europe."

"Why are you telling me any of this?" Yona asked.

"I don't want you to lose hope."

"I have God. Jesus is my hope. With Him, I never lose hope." Yona knew she was coming on strong with her statement, but there it was.

"God is my hope too." Dmitri motioned for her to pick any seat she wanted.

Yona sat down away from the door.

Dmitri followed her. "Kelvin asked about you. He was concerned."

"About what?" Yona hadn't spoken to Kelvin since they were both at Reuel's castle.

"He thinks you're going after Ulysses to get to Reuel."

"You are too," Yona said. "So are Dario and Leland."

"Leland's in the machine room with Cayson back in Atlanta, but yes, we're all going after Aspasia and Ulysses."

Yona heard voices outside the conference room. Someone laughing alone.

She turned to Dmitri. "If you see Kelvin again, please tell him not to worry, but pray to God instead."

Dmitri nodded.

Yona did not recognize the woman entering the

room as she put away her phone. She was carrying a tablet in her other hand.

"Espy, come meet Yona Epstein." Dmitri got up from his seat to retrieve a remote control from a side cabinet.

The woman came around the table to shake Yona's hand. "Esperanza Diaz-Mendenhall. Nice to meet you."

"Same."

"Espy runs Watchfire Security. Today we're going to test a joint operation," Dmitri said. "If it works out, I'm selling my security company to her."

Yona raised her eyebrows.

"I'm retiring. My farm animals need me." Dmitri looked away at the wall. "My daughter needs me."

"She's thirty-three, at least." Esperanza smiled.

"I haven't been there for her since birth."

"I'm sorry. Must be hard. I'll take good care of your Sentinels, Inc." Esperanza sat down. "And you're still going to be our advisor."

"What are you going to call the new company?" Yona asked.

"Watchfire Security." Esperanza looked at Yona. "You Mossad?"

"Former. I retired." Yona guessed that Esperanza probably knew that and more.

"Dmitri speaks highly of you," Esperanza said.

"We just met two weeks ago." Yona glanced at Dmitri and found him chuckling.

"We might have," he said. "But I've known about you for a long time."

"Since when?" Yona asked.

"Issachar and I go way back." Dmitri sighed. "Before he turned."

"Did they bury him a second time?" Esperanza asked.

"His body was never found." Yona thought that was unusual as well. She had been the only witness outside of Reuel's circle. Perhaps Issachar was still alive. Who knew?

"How's Kelvin?" Esperanza's eyes were still on Yona.

See, she knows too much.

"According to Dmitri, he's hanging in there," Yona replied. "I haven't seen him myself."

"Not once?"

"No. I don't see any reason to do so." Yona tapped the table with her fingers. "My goal here is to find Aspasia and Ulysses. Their testimonies could help reduce Kelvin's sentencing."

"I agree." Dmitri pushed a button on his remote. A screen came down from the ceiling in front of them. "Let's get started."

Esperanza swiped her tablet. It connected to the larger screen. She showed a few slides of burning buildings. "Tel Aviv, five years ago. Molyneux's handiwork."

Yona remembered. "I was there, helping out wherever we could."

"We never met," Esperanza said. "It was tough for your country."

Yona nodded. "For every country in Molyneux's path. Glad she's in prison now."

"For the rest of her life. But it took a while to catch her. Years." Esperanza played a news clip.

Yona watched a tour bus burn in Vienna.

"This was five miles from here," Esperanza explained. "One sunny December day three years ago, my team and I were still hunting for Molyneux."

Dmitri offered the ladies bottled water. "Cold, pure spring water."

Yona thanked him. "She might be gone, but her remnants are still around."

"I can't believe Ulysses took over MedusaNet," Esperanza said.

"And renamed it Telemachus," Yona reminded everyone.

"He was in Project Pericarp, wasn't he?"

Yona nodded. "I was an observer. I didn't

interact much with him then. I didn't know about Aspasia until she showed up in Prague last month."

Dmitri rubbed his temple. "I mentored Ulysses. I brought him into the project as an independent contractor. I vouched for him. Everything he knew, he learned from me."

"It's not your fault." Esperanza's voice was cold.

"Ulysses had five heart attacks by the time he was fifty-five. You'd think he'd take it easy, but no."

Yona felt sorry for the poor man. "He was so deep in the project that he decided it was worth throwing away his entire life to take over a crime syndicate?"

"A global terrorist organization. He thinks there's glory in there somewhere." Dmitri shook his head.

"Yeah. It happens. People can change for the worse," Esperanza said. "Kelvin is the guy I don't understand. He was the system administrator at Binary Systems. He wasn't in Project Pericarp directly."

"He knew all about it, though," Yona said. "They heavily used the Binary Systems computers and networks. Kelvin was the one in charge of those systems. He kept them running twenty-four seven. Everyone knew him. If we needed computer help, we'd go to him. He was our tech support."

"And no one had any idea that he was also a hacker by trade," Esperanza said.

"A burned-out hacker who found system administration more his type of work."

"Yet, when Aspasia hired him, all he did was hack."

Dmitri laughed. "Money can make people do anything, Espy. Money. And money has brought Ulysses back to Vienna."

Dmitri drank more water. "Our contacts told us that he has called several of Molyneux's associates who were left high and dry after she went to prison. He wanted them to know they can be back in business again."

"Ulysses doesn't know how I look or who I am," Esperanza said. "I'm meeting him at a coffeehouse. It shouldn't be hard for me to put on a Spanish accent, considering I was born in Barcelona, and worked for years in Madrid."

"What's my role?" Yona hoped she hadn't flown all the way here just to sit behind a monitor.

"You sit behind a monitor with me," Dmitri replied.

What did I say?

"And sip coffee—or tea, whatever your preference—while we watch Espy there handcuff Ulysses."

"They won't let us do that in broad daylight." Esperanza laughed.

"I'd like to be closer to the coffeehouse," Yona said. "Maybe I can help somehow."

"You want to sit in a crammed van all day long in the sunny month of June?" Esperanza asked.

Yona nodded.

"It's going to be very hot." Esperanza swiped her tablet again. "Ninety degrees this entire week. No rain."

Yona nodded again.

"You got it then. Let's go."

CHAPTER TWENTY-TWO

Vienna was all sunshine and no clouds that afternoon when Esperanza and one of her men—both of them wearing wigs and hats—went to the outdoor coffeehouse to meet someone they thought would be Ulysses.

One block away, inside a utility van, Yona sat between two operators. On one screen were video images coming from the camera sewn into Esperanza's vest. The other screen showed video from a camera that must have been on top of a pole or something.

Yona watched the stranger sit down on the other side of the table. He did not look like Ulysses at all. Granted, Ulysses might have colored his hair, but the man was at least fifty years old. This guy's hands were smooth and taut.

"That's not Ulysses." Yona had to say it but she didn't want to overstep her boundaries.

"You sure?" One of the operators asked her to confirm.

"I know it has been three or four years, but if I remember correctly, Ulysses had a jutted chin."

"He got a chin job?"

"Maybe. But that guy's eyes are smaller."

"Plastic surgery?"

"Or he might have sent someone else," Yona suggested.

Everyone concurred with her.

Really, she should not interfere in the operation. It wasn't hers to begin with. She was only there as an observer, yet again.

Still, she had worn her hiking boots and tied up her hair into a bun under a baseball cap, just in case she had to go out there for some reason.

Through the two screens, Yona could see that the discussion was turning sour. The man was no longer smiling. In fact, he got up to walk away.

He passed by a single woman sitting three tables away. Neither looked at each other.

There was something about that woman...

"Could you zoom in to that woman sitting

alone at the table? Floral dress? Brown hair?" Yona asked.

One of the operators did.

"Whoa." Yona was out of the van before anyone could stop her.

She saw Esperanza following the man down the street.

Yona walked quickly toward the woman at the table, and sat down on the other chair. "Hello, Aspasia."

She didn't reply.

"Still looking for Ulysses?" Yona asked.

No answer.

"Did you know he just walked past you?" Yona remembered telling the operators in the van that she didn't think it was Ulysses, but she was fishing now for confirmation.

The woman looked startled and almost turned her head. "Why are you here?"

"We'll talk later. He's leaving the store right now."

They both got up at once.

Aspasia was faster.

The man started to run.

Aspasia went after him. So did Yona, Esperanza and just about everyone in the operation.

Esperanza sprinted by Yona. "Didn't I tell you to stay out of this?"

They nearly caught up with the man who suddenly pulled out a pistol—

"He's got a gun, Espy!"

And he was pointing in Yona's direction.

Or was it at Aspasia?

Yona tackled Aspasia and pushed her to the ground as she heard the sound of a single gunshot.

Thousands of feet stampeded around them as Yona and Aspasia hid under a table.

"You do this often?" Aspasia asked.

"Only when I need a witness." Yona realized she had no weapons. She had her cell phone with her, but she didn't have Esperanza's number.

When the noise died down a bit, Yona lifted the bottom edge of the tablecloth to peek out. "Coast is clear."

She crawled out and pulled Aspasia to her feet.

"He shot at me." Aspasia was holding back tears.

"It could've been meant for the rest of us."

"I don't know."

"Besides, he didn't look like Ulysses." Yona saw that the local Prague police were helping Esperanza and Ben apprehend the man, whose wig had fallen off.

"Oh yes. That was him." Aspasia burst into tears. "After all these years, he shot at me."

She rushed forward to kick Ulysses, but a police officer held her back.

"Fight him in court," a tourist said within earshot.

"I will!" Aspasia replied. She turned to Yona. "You said you need a witness?"

"Yes."

"You got yourself a witness."

CHAPTER TWENTY-THREE

Upon the advice of Dmitri and Esperanza, Yona did not appear in person to support Kelvin in his court case. None of them could show their faces in public. If Dario were in town, he would have done the same.

Poor Kelvin.

Yona had asked his lawyer to tell him that they were praying for him, for a speedy trial and for God's perfect will to be done in his life.

She didn't have to say that it wasn't God's perfect will that Kelvin committed multiple crimes. However, now that he had done them all, he had to pay for them.

At least some of them.

The severity of his punishment would be counterbalanced by not only his actions for the greater good but also by Aspasia's scathing testimony of what Ulysses had made her do. Hiring Kelvin was one thing, but forcing him to work for the terrorists was another thing.

To take her mind off the matter, Yona did what she had promised Kelvin: take care of his cat.

Her hotel was only five or six blocks away, so she decided to walk. On the way there, she stopped at a corner store to buy cat food. She remembered Kelvin saying that Mordecai liked mackerel, tuna, or shrimp. She bought all three.

When she arrived at the abandoned building where she had first found Kelvin a month ago, she realized that the building had a new coat of paint. Perhaps it was finally sold.

She knocked on the door of the smaller house next to it.

After a while, someone cracked a nearby window slightly and looked at her through rusty metal scrollwork.

Her face was wrinkled and her eyelids drooped.

"Tereza?" Yona asked.

The old lady nodded.

Using an English-Czech translator app on her

phone, Yona said, "Hello, I'm Yona. I told Kelvin that I would check on his cat."

Yona pointed her phone in Tereza's direction so that the translator could pick up her words.

"He is still here," Tereza said. Or rather, the translator did.

"The cat?"

Tereza nodded.

"He is eight years old, and I don't let him go out anymore."

Eight years? Not too old for a cat. "Why?"

"Because if he disappears, then when Kelvin comes out of jail, he will be sad." The woman spoke so quickly that she had to repeat for Yona's translator app to catch every word.

"I brought some cat food." Yona lifted a paper sack for her to see.

"Thank you," Tereza said in English after listening to the translator app. "Wait there."

Minutes later, Tereza came to the door, opened it, and invited Yona into her cramped living room, where the furniture looked as old as the house.

By the window, there was a sliver of afternoon sunlight tracking across the wooden floor. Right in the middle of that sunshine—filtered through a sheer curtain—Mordecai was sleeping, legs spread out.

His fur was mostly gray, with white speckles under his chin and on his belly.

His eyes opened, and they were green.

"Do you want to feed him yourself?" Tereza pointed to two bowls near a wall. One had water in it, and the other was empty.

Yona hated seeing it empty.

"Are you hungry?" Yona waved a can in front of the cat.

Mordecai ignored her.

"We can feed him later. He will tell us when he is hungry," Tereza said.

"How?"

"He will make a lot of noise. You will hear it." She pointed to a couch. "Please, sit down. I will bring you some tea."

"Thank you." Yona found a clean spot and sat down on the couch.

She didn't know what else to do other than to watch the cat sleep.

Every now and then Mordecai lifted his head to look at her.

Slowly, he got up, and rubbed his neck against Yona's calves. Then he climbed onto the couch and started to knead the cushion. He curled up next to Yona and went to sleep.

"I think we made a connection," Yona said to no one.

Hot tea came.

"Do you have family?" Yona asked through her phone translator.

"Two sons. They moved away," she said quietly. "I may need to move too."

"Why?"

"I can no longer afford this house. My son has been paying for this house, but his company is not doing well this year."

Yona didn't ask what his son did. It was none of her business.

However, the house...

"Are you selling the house?" Yona asked.

"I have thought of it, but for now, I'll take tenants."

"How old is this house?"

"Three hundred years old."

"Wow." Yona was thinking there'd be a lot of germs in this house.

"I want to rent the upstairs rooms out because I cannot climb the stairs anymore."

That got Yona thinking. Working for Dmitri, she was location independent. She could live in Prague, couldn't she? She'd have to get a long-term visa or residency permit. Perhaps she could test out a visit first.

She could have stayed in Vienna after they captured Aspasia and Ulysses. However, those two people had been sent to the International Criminal Court in The Hague. It was a slightly different court than where Kelvin was today.

"I don't know how long I will be here," Yona said. "But maybe I can rent a room upstairs for three months."

Ninety days should be enough.

After that, she could either go home to Israel or see where Dmitri wanted her to work next.

CHAPTER TWENTY-FOUR

For the next three years, every Tuesday night before the lights were turned off in his cell, Kelvin found himself writing another letter to Yona.

Sometimes the letters were short—just a couple of sentences. Sometimes they were long.

Once a week, without fail, he'd write to her.

After collecting a month's worth of letters—four a month—he would send the bulk mail to a post office box that Dmitri had designated in Vienna. And he would not call her by her name, only an initial.

Truth be told, he couldn't be sure Yona had read any of his letters, because she rarely replied except for the cards that she sent at Christmas, Easter, Thanksgiving, and on his birthday.

She said in one of her earlier letters that she had asked Leland about celebrations and holidays in the USA so that she could send him some encouragement.

Kelvin would rather that Yona wrote more frequently, but he knew that working for Dmitri might muzzle her freedom. To protect her anonymity in town and elsewhere, Yona could not visit him at the prison.

Perhaps it also followed that she sent him infrequent cards that had no return address.

Tonight, Kelvin couldn't finish his letter. Something bothered him, distracted him. That something was a card he had received that afternoon.

He pulled out the card from the back of his Bible.

It was from Reuel, the one who got away three years before. The one whom Yona could still be looking for.

How are you? Hope you're well.

Kelvin hardly knew the man except for those weeks Kelvin had been held captive in the castle outside Prague, when Reuel had forced him and his colleagues to hijack the new network that Ulysses was trying to use to run his underground operations.

Kelvin was glad he had helped thwart Ulysses's plan to become the next Molyneux. That had reduced his prison time.

Aspasia and Molyneux now shared the same prison location outside Vienna, while no one knew where they had taken Ulysses.

Word was that the FSB wanted to talk to him. Didn't they want to talk to Reuel too?

Kelvin wondered how to tell Dmitri that Reuel knew where Kelvin was.

Would it even matter to Dmitri if I live or die?

That was a good question.

He put Reuel's card into the envelope meant for Yona's letter, and sealed it. Then he decided not to send it. He put the sealed envelope back into the back flaps of his worn Bible.

The lights went out before he could return to his letter to Yona. Just as well. He couldn't remember what he wanted to say to her tonight.

To make it worse, he had been so distracted by Reuel's card that he forgot to read his Bible. Now it was too dark.

He stretched out on his hard bed. No roommates. No one else there but occasional rats that scurried about.

He was used to rats since they were the same type of rats as in that abandoned building in Prague he had hidden in three years before.

Staring at the dark ceiling, he tried to recall the verses he'd read that morning. He had read 1 John 1:8-9 so many times that he had decided to memorize it.

> *If we say that we have no sin, we deceive ourselves, and the truth is not in us. If we confess our sins, He is faithful and just to forgive us our sins and to cleanse us from all unrighteousness.*

Kelvin had asked multiple times for God to forgive him. Sometimes he didn't feel like he had been forgiven of his sins, but that verse assured him that he had to put aside his feelings and trust God by faith. If God said He would forgive him of his sins, He would.

Kelvin closed his eyes and prayed for everyone on his daily prayer list. Primarily, he prayed for Yona, Leland, Cayson, Dmitri, and Dario. Not having any family of his own, these people at his work were his family.

Before he could say amen, he fell asleep peacefully.

CHAPTER TWENTY-FIVE

A few weeks later, Kelvin was glad he hadn't sent Reuel's card to Dmitri.

One fine day, while he was busy living his life in solitary confinement, the CIA showed up at the prison to see him.

Dario de la Cruz hadn't come alone. His colleague only introduced himself as Leonid, but he was clearly FSB.

Kelvin could see all sorts of leverage there with the way the FSB had treated him three years before.

"Two years off?" Kelvin leaned against the table, his handcuffs tapping the stainless-steel top.

"Up to two years," Dario corrected him.

Two years of reduction in his sentence meant

Kelvin could be out in eight years. However, the things they wanted him to do didn't justify such a small compensation.

He prayed silently for wisdom to negotiate. Somehow, he wanted them to do something for him with regard to Reuel, in addition to reducing his prison sentence.

He glanced over at his not-so-silent multilingual attorney, whom Dmitri had sent. She was writing something on her tablet.

"What are you asking my client to do for you again?" Barbara Nováková asked.

Dario listed it.

Leonid added a few more to the list.

By the time they finished, Kelvin's attorney had swiped her tablet at least twice.

Kelvin mulled over the situation. He was surprised that the CIA needed him for this. And that. And then some.

"Why didn't you ask Binary Systems to help you?" Kelvin asked Dario.

"They are busy. You're closest to the fire."

"That's how you get third-degree burns." Kelvin looked at Leonid, who didn't reply. Surely he had known Kelvin's history with the FSB.

The fact that Leonid had not said anything so

far told Kelvin a lot. It seemed to him that they would rather not have asked Kelvin for help at all.

However, he was the only one who knew more about Ulysses's operations than anyone else alive today. Reuel might know, but he had been missing for three years.

"Please think about this," Dario said. "Ulysses won't talk. We believe he's still in control. He has got to have someone on the outside running the show on his behalf. As long as he's still operating, we're all still in danger, including Leland, Cayson, Yona, and you."

Yona.

Kelvin tried not to freak out. He'd do anything to protect Yona. And Dario knew that.

"I need to confer with my client," Nováková said. "Could you wait outside for ten minutes?"

The agents nodded and left the room.

"Five more years instead of seven if you take their offer. Can you handle five?" Nováková asked. "You've already been in here for three."

"They're asking a lot. If I succeed, Ulysses's people will come after me and I could lose my life. So two years off are insufficient."

Nováková nodded.

"Even though the Telemachus network is shut down, and both Ulysses and Aspasia are serving time, along with Molyneux, there are others willing to take their places. Those are the people I fear more."

Kelvin knew he should only fear God, but the threats of Ulysses's successors were a big unknown at this point. His life could be in the balance.

"So we need them to set you free sooner."

"What about house arrest?" Kelvin asked. "With an ankle monitor, they'll know where I am at all times."

"Right. So maybe one more year in here and two years of house arrest. You probably can't leave Prague."

"I don't mind that," Kelvin said. "However, I want to be allowed out once a week to go to the theater or walk along the river."

"They'll probably have to send a guard. All that costs money."

"Make the CIA and FSB pay for it." Kelvin was confident they'd agree.

Nováková nodded. "They really need you, don't they?"

"Yes. If they won't let me out in five years, what then?"

"Technically, you won't be out. You'll still be in prison—if house arrest is a form of prison. They might even require you to work for the CIA and you can't do anything else."

Kelvin realized they were discussing his freedom.

How far have I fallen!

As a kid so many years ago, he hadn't realized how precious his freedom was. Now that he had lost it...

"I'd rather stay here one more year if it means I can get more freedom afterwards," he said.

"Perhaps if you stay here for five years in total, and they let you out for two years under a modified house arrest in which you will be allowed to walk about within the city, with no access to the internet except when you're working for the CIA or FSB."

"Or for Dmitri Proskouriakoff. His company is a contractor for the CIA, and he was former FSB, although he defected to the USA a very long time ago. Find out if I can work for him while under house arrest."

"In Prague."

Kelvin nodded.

"That's a lot of freedom. You're supposed to be a prisoner."

"Do they want Ulysses's cohorts or not?"

"Good point." Nováková smiled.

"One more thing." Kelvin decided to play his

trump card. "On top of all that, I want them to promise to do whatever they need to find Reuel."

"Who?"

Kelvin told his attorney about Reuel. "He disappeared three years ago, as far as I know. As long as he is still out there, a person dear to me could be in danger. I want the CIA and FSB to find him and get him out of the way. In return I will do whatever they ask me to do related to Ulysses."

Eliminating Ulysses's threat would also protect Yona.

"Is this person still alive?" Nováková asked. "You said he's been missing for three years."

"Oh yeah. He's still around." Kelvin produced the envelope from his pocket. He tore it and handed the card to his attorney.

"It's just a card."

"To you it is, but to Dario et al., it says that Reuel knew which prison I'm in—even though nothing was said in the news—and he was able to get a message to me. The note is benign on the surface, but he wants me to know he is still around."

"So? You're safe here."

"He also knows that the woman I love is out there."

"Then we do whatever we can to get a win-win situation."

"Thank you. That's all I ask."

Irony of ironies. Thanks to Ulysses, Aspasia, and Molyneux still being alive, their presence in this world meant that Kelvin was still useful to the authorities who wanted to destroy their terrorist organizations.

He was still needed by the governments who had once abandoned him to the wolves.

"You're tougher than I thought," Nováková said.

"I've had three years to toughen up. If I am not tough, I'd perish in this prison." Kelvin looked at his attorney kindly. "Thank you for letting me get solitary confinement. You saved my sanity."

"Thank God. It was a miracle they agreed."

"Yes, thank God indeed. Even in my pit of despair, He is with me."

Nováková glanced at her watch. "It's more than ten minutes."

She motioned for the guard to let Dario and Leonid back into the room while Kelvin silently prayed that the CIA and FSB would agree to their counteroffer.

It was indeed a win-win plan, but Kelvin didn't

want to think about the fact that he had more to lose overall if they decided not to go for it.

It would mean ten total years in this prison.

Ten years of solitary confinement writing letters that nobody might read.

He had served three years, but seven more years would mean he'd be forty-two years old when they let him out.

By then, his faithful cat, Mordecai, could be dead.

And Yona could have moved on. She deserved to move on.

Kelvin blinked away a tear.

CHAPTER TWENTY-SIX

Yona's initial ninety days of renting a room from Tereza turned into twelve months, and twelve months turned into three years, until that day Yona received word that Kelvin had started cooperating with the CIA and FSB in their joint operation.

Three years then turned into five, with Yona busy working for Dmitri, flying everywhere with him to various places in Europe, from Prague to Vienna to Paris and then back to Prague.

Dmitri had established more projects in Europe for the computer company he co-owned. While his business partner focused on business in North America, Dmitri chose to expand their division in Europe.

So much for Dmitri's desire to retire.

And he wanted Yona close by. Treating her more like a daughter than an employee, Dmitri had shown her more favor than any of her previous mentors.

Yona was careful not to overstep her boundaries. She knew that Dmitri had a daughter living in the United States. Any day now, the daughter could take over his operations.

For now, Dmitri did what Dmitri wanted.

It made sense for Dmitri to be headquartered in Prague. The office building was nice, and Yona liked walking or cycling to work. She didn't even own a car.

Sometimes Yona had to work on weekends, but not today. The morning air was cool, and she wanted to walk before the sun warmed up this Saturday in June.

She hadn't heard from Kelvin in a few months. The agencies worked him hard. He had told her in his letters that he wanted to work hard. The more he worked, the more years they would take off his incarceration.

Yona had no idea when he would get out of jail. It had been a very long five years. He still had another three years left to go, even with all the sentence reduction.

Sometimes she wondered if she should move on from Kelvin. There were some cute guys at Dmitri's office who were interested in her. She had gone out with one or two of them in the last three years, but it hadn't worked out.

It didn't help that all she could think of was that she'd better wait for Kelvin.

Sitting on a bench outside Tereza's house, Yona laced up her favorite pair of hiking boots. Those soles could handle the cobblestone sidewalks better than her regular walking shoes. She preferred walking because she could slow down by the river and take in the scenery, especially at this time of the day before the tourists flooded the city.

She wished she had a walking companion. However, her work kept her too busy to make friends. When she had free time, she would take Tereza to the doctor, to run errands, to go shopping, and so forth.

Yona felt sorry for her because her children hadn't come back to visit her in three years. In a way, Yona had become her surrogate daughter.

It was fine with Yona because she needed something to occupy her free time, in addition to reading books.

Being single was both easy and hard. Easy to schedule anything on a whim because she alone made all the decisions. Hard because she felt lonely sometimes.

Very lonely.

Sometimes she wished she dared to write a letter to Kelvin. Or that he would write her as frequently as he used to do in his first three years behind bars.

Had Kelvin moved on from her? Perhaps whatever they'd almost had was in the past, except for Mordecai the cat—once a street cat, now a pampered house cat.

For the last five years, Yona had taken care of that senior cat. She took him to the veterinarian. She trimmed his nails, combed his hair, sang to him, and fed him all his favorite foods.

Walking along Vltava River, under those pretty streetlights, Yona passed by people jogging in pairs. Some of them looked happy together.

Yona still didn't speak Czech, but some of the joggers spoke English. She didn't mean to listen in, but she wasn't wearing her earbuds. She wanted to immerse herself in the real-life environment she was in.

People came here for vacations. And she had lived here for five years.

She checked her watch and quickened her

strides. Turning onto Charles Bridge, she came to a complete stop.

There, standing in front of her, was none other than Kelvin Gallagher.

Stunned, she had no words.

Clean shaven, he was in a pair of jeans and a distressed T-shirt.

Please don't tell me you broke out of prison. "What are you doing here?"

"Meeting Dmitri." He glanced at the tall man standing next to him. The man nodded.

Was he a guard? Yona couldn't tell. "Dmitri? That can't be right. He's in Paris today."

"For real? I received a message after they let me out that I am to meet him here at nine o'clock," Kelvin answered. "Do you think he forgot?"

"No. That's not possible. Unless..."

Kelvin laughed. "Unless he set us up."

The man next to him frowned.

"Considering I walk at this time on Saturdays," Yona said.

"Alone?"

"Alone." Yona realized that she had become too predictable these days. She should change up her schedule so that no one could be expecting her at precisely the same location at the same time ever week.

"I gather Dmitri is not coming." Kelvin grinned.

"You gather right."

"May I walk with you then?" Kelvin asked.

"Out here in the open?" Yona wondered.

"Dmitri didn't tell you?"

"Tell me what?"

"Because of the amazing work I have done for various you-know-what entities, they are allowing me to serve the remainder of my sentence at home."

"House arrest?" In exchange for lending his expertise to the CIA, FBI, NSA, MI6, INTER-POL, and other government entities.

"I can't go past the city limits though, and I have an ankle band." Kelvin lifted the hem of his jeans to show her his ankle monitor.

Yona pointed to the guy who had accompanied Kelvin to the bridge. "Who is he then?"

"He's here to make sure nobody takes me out."

Yona thought that made sense because Kelvin had made enough enemies over the years. Thanks to Yona's report, the Mossad didn't consider Kelvin an enemy though.

Speaking of the Mossad, Yona hadn't received a single word about Reuel. Five years. Where could he have been? Dead, perhaps?

Dmitri had promised to help her hunt him down. How long was this going to take them?

"Well, Kelvin, here we are on an open bridge," Yona asked. "Is this a good idea?"

"I wanted to see you right away. I'm on my way to my new apartment—flat."

"You can't leave town," Yona repeated. *What kind of a non-freedom was that?*

"But I can invite you to a concert in town if we want to go." Kelvin paused. "If you don't have other plans. Or anyone."

"No one. Dmitri has kept me so busy the last five years that work was all I did most of the time." Yona said it without hesitation, surprising even herself. "I would love to go to a concert with you."

"Classical or jazz?"

"Classical."

"Have you eaten breakfast?"

"Not yet."

"Coffee or tea?"

"Tea." Yona smiled. "What are you up to, Kelvin?"

Kelvin stepped forward. "I've prayed about this for the last several years. Altogether I've waited for nine years to ask you out. If I don't ask now... God hasn't promised us tomorrow."

"Didn't I say yes to a tea and concert?"

"I know. It feels surreal that you would."

"Why wouldn't I?"

"Because I'm still a convict. I'll be a convict for the next three years."

Yona reached for his hand. "Five years passed by quickly. The next three years might fly by too."

"I've dreamed of this moment for a long time." Kelvin lifted her hand. "Do you remember when we were in Reuel's castle?"

Yona nodded. At their meals three times a day, Yona and Kelvin had conversed and plotted their escape. They had whispered in each other's ears.

"Five years ago, and it's still vivid in my mind," she said.

"I remember how much I wanted to..." He eyed Yona's lips.

She knew that he wanted her to respond. She ran a finger across his chin. "I'm glad you shaved."

As he smiled, she pressed her lips against his chin. Then the edge of his lips.

Suddenly realizing their guard was watching them, she stopped.

Kelvin took over, molding his lips on Yona's. His lips felt supple and smooth. And tasted like fresh toothpaste and clean water.

I like a clean man.

He was a good kisser.

But did he have a good heart?

The kiss ended too quickly. Kelvin wrapped his arms around Yona.

It was the first time they'd finally kissed. And the first time they'd hugged.

It felt good.

Funny how a word could trigger a memory. Yona recalled a verse she had memorized. Luke 18:19.

> *So Jesus said to him, "Why do you call Me good?*
> *No one is good but One, that is, God..."*

Only God was good.

Man was sinful and continued to battle his sin nature for the rest of his life on earth.

Then again, God called His people to do good deeds in Luke 19:17.

> *And he said to him, "Well done, good servant;*
> *because you were faithful in a very little, have*
> *authority over ten cities."*

Yona prayed that she and Kelvin would be faithful to God over everything.

"I have something to share with you," Kelvin said.

Yona waited.

"I have a long way to go, far beyond the next years," Kelvin said.

"Okay. Shall we walk?" Yona held his hand and led him down the bridge and along the river.

"I've been studying the Bible a lot. I've been reading through the Bible every year, memorizing key passages."

"That's impressive. I want to read through my Bible every year, but I haven't actually done it."

"It's refreshing to read His Word daily."

"Right."

"Speaking for myself, if I want to be a better Christian, I must spend time in God's Word. Only He can teach me about Himself."

"Good."

"I want to be the best man God created me to be—in spite of my past sins."

"We have all sinned, as you know. We are all still learning."

Kelvin nodded. "Someday, I also hope to be the best husband God can make me."

Husband?

When you know, you know.

"What do you think about my goals?" Kelvin asked.

"As with all noble goals, only God can help you get there."

"True."

"I will pray for God's perfect will to prevail in your life...and mine too." She hadn't let go of his hand.

"Good prayer." He lifted her chin. "You haven't changed in all these years. Your face is still as lovely as ever."

"It's not me." She laughed. "I believe in Jesus. I have peace with God."

"I can see the peace of God in your face."

"Yours too. You have come to an understanding. You look like you do have the peace of God in your heart."

Kelvin's eyes teared up. "I have asked God to forgive me. I am halfway through reaping what I sowed. But my soul is well. I am finally at peace with God."

Kelvin had grown so much spiritually. Perhaps that had been why God had allowed him to be punished for his crimes this way. In jail, he'd had time to study God's Word and prepare for life outside of prison.

Yona couldn't speak. She wanted to cry, but no tears came.

Kelvin leaned toward her ear and whispered, "I love you."

Yona's lips trembled.

And he calmed her with another kiss.

Those warm lips.

She felt she could get used to it. "Do that every day?"

"Tell you I love you and kiss you?"

Yona nodded, tears welling in her eyes.

"Yes, for the rest of my life."

CHAPTER TWENTY-SEVEN

The more Kelvin assisted law enforcement agencies in Europe, the United Kingdom, and the United States, the more prison time he was able to chip away. As another year progressed, he became more confident that it would be over soon.

Then he could fly home to the United States to put some flowers on his mother's grave.

His modified house arrest was going well. It was the best deal his attorney could negotiate for him. Five years served in prison and two years under house arrest.

The last two years of his five years at the prison had been some of his busiest years. If the CIA didn't want something from him, the FSB did. If neither did, then MI6 or INTERPOL had questions. And the cycle continued for twenty-four months.

And then he was under house arrest.

That was a big deal to Kelvin because he could work for Dmitri—right in the same office that Yona worked in. Dmitri had vouched for him, which meant all the world to Kelvin.

Every day, as long as he was either at his small flat or at Dmitri's office complex, he was fine. Once a week, he could take Yona out to a dinner and theater or concert. Other days, he ate his meals either at work or at his apartment. They let him walk along the river and on the bridges as long as he didn't leave the Prague city limits.

In spite of all that, he still had to check in with his CIA handler every day, not to mention his assigned prison officer. He got used to that fast, because breathing fresh air out here was better than inhaling stale air inside that prison, as historic as the place might be.

The rest of the time, Kelvin was busy working for Dmitri, who had feelers in many governments. Even though he had rounded up Ulysses's colleagues for the CIA and FSB, they still called him for other things. It gave Kelvin a chance to ask them if they had found Reuel.

Speaking of Dmitri, he had moved his entire European operation to Prague. His business partner remained in the States, but Dmitri hardly went home anymore.

Kelvin liked Dmitri's new office complex in Prague. He could see Yona almost daily. Sometimes several times a day when she was in town.

This early spring morning was special because Kelvin had finished praying about it and felt in his heart that the timing was right.

It had been right for a while now.

He was especially grateful to God that Yona agreed to have dinner with him once a week. Sometimes they ate lunch together at the office. Takeout from the cafeteria.

Yona had given Kelvin the impression that they were an item. He enjoyed their strolls by the river and the sweet kisses that followed.

Yona had not judged him based on his criminal past, but had been fair to him. She had focused on his present-day redemption and what he did with the second chance that God had given him to lead a new life.

Kelvin wasn't going to let God down.

Or Yona. Who respected him as a human being, in spite of his past foibles and foolishness.

Kelvin could tell that Yona had warmed up to

him over the past year, not because they were two lonely people in Prague or that they had a history together, but perhaps because they both wanted to start over and have new lives.

And at this moment in time, God had seen fit to bring them together.

There must be something more than coffee and kisses.

Would she have kissed someone she disliked? Probably not.

Kelvin glanced at the clock. It was 7:50 a.m.

Five more minutes and Yona should be coming through the elevator doors and heading to her office.

At precisely 8:00 a.m., she would be at her desk, logging in to her computer.

Kelvin wondered how she would react to the multicolored tulips on her desk and the note he'd left for her. He had bought the flowers and delivered them himself.

Kelvin started to get nervous, which was highly unusual.

He hadn't been nervous when they sentenced him to ten years of prison. He hadn't been nervous when his cooperation from behind prison walls reduced his sentence to five years in jail and three years of house arrest.

Now he was nervous to the bones.

The elevator door opened.

7:55 a.m.

Kelvin braced himself.

From his cubicle, he had a direct view of the hallway and the bank of glass walls. In the middle of the row of offices, Yona unlocked her door. She was carrying a cup of coffee in her hand and a backpack on her back.

She was dressed in all black leather, and her hair was tied up in a bun behind her head. She was dressed to leave.

Kelvin's heart sank. He was hoping to talk things out at lunch, but she looked like she might not have time for him today.

Yona put the coffee down and stared at the flowers. She opened the envelope and pulled out the note.

Kelvin held his breath.

She turned and faced the glass wall and looked directly at Kelvin.

He froze.

He shouldn't have been staring. Now he had no chance to pretend like he wasn't.

Yona crossed the hallway in her combat boots, Kelvin's note in her hand.

Her lips reached his before their arms intertwined.

There must be some office policy, but Kelvin couldn't remember what.

When she came up for air, she said, "My answer is yes. Now ask me properly."

Kelvin looked around. There were at least half a dozen people staring at them.

"Now?" Kelvin could feel the shudder in his own voice. "I was going to ask you at lunch."

"I'm leaving in thirty minutes." Yona stepped back. "If you don't ask me face to face, is it even valid?"

"In private?"

Yona waved her arms. "There is no privacy here. It's an open space."

"Uh..."

"It's okay if you want to wait three months."

"Is that how long you'll be gone?"

Yona nodded. "Or longer."

This is it! Help me, Lord.

Kelvin knelt down on one knee. A ring magically appeared in his hand. Actually, he had somehow retrieved it from his pocket, but he couldn't remember when he did that exactly.

"Yona Epstein," Kelvin said. "You're the most forgiving person I know apart from Jesus. You look past my sins and see what God could make of me. You helped me to see my potential in Christ. Much more than that, you waited for me all these years and listened to me when I shared with you all my fears and failures."

Tears streamed down Yona's cheeks.

"Even after knowing all about me, you still went out with me. Even when all I could afford was an apple strudel to share between us or homemade sandwich or merely walks by the river."

Yona wiped her eyes.

"I enjoy spending time with you, and I want to be with you the rest of my life, however long or short a time God gives us. Will you share my life with me? Will you be my wife and walk with me through life?"

Yona nodded.

"I promise to love you all the days of my life—through happy and hard times, through good times and bad. Will you marry me, Yona Epstein?"

Yona drew a deep breath. "Yes, again."

It was a good thing that Kelvin had prepared her by popping the question—albeit abridged—in the note that went with the flowers. If she had decided not to accept him, she wouldn't have come across the hallway to make him ask in person.

It would have spared both of them any embarrassment, as the question wouldn't have been asked aloud.

Here they were.

Kelvin nearly dropped the ring as he slid it onto Yona's ring finger.

"When do we marry?" Yona asked.

"In a hurry, are we?" Kelvin handed her a tissue paper to wipe the tears from her eyes. She seemed to be wearing some makeup that Kelvin didn't want to mess. He wasn't sure how one wiped tears from a face that had makeup on it.

He stared.

He had never seen Yona so moved as when she looked at the ring on her finger.

He had saved up all year to buy this ring. The diamond was small, but he'd paid cash for it.

"We're not promised tomorrow. You've heard the expression before."

"My ankle monitor comes off in about ten months. After that, I get to travel." *Maybe even go home to the United States.*

"A simple wedding won't take long to prepare." Yona pulled Kelvin to his feet.

"A spring wedding then."

Yona nodded as she ran a finger across Kelvin's lips.

Their kiss was short lived.

Applause interrupted their brief celebration.

"Congratulations!" Dmitri came up to them. His eyes were on Kelvin. "Very clever, Kel."

"What?" Yona's eyebrows rose.

"He popped the question before he told you about the other thing," Dmitri said.

"What other thing?" Yona's fists were on her hips now.

"Reuel is in custody." Dmitri smiled.

"Seriously?" Yona's head swung toward Kelvin so fast that it stunned him. "How?"

"You'll have to ask the CIA and FSB, but I doubt they'd give you great details," Kelvin said. "Just thank God it's all over. We're safe now."

"Reuel. After six years." Yona exhaled.

"He was hard to find," Dmitri said. "He had plastic surgery and moved to Brazil. He went off the grid. Never left the house he stayed in. If not for the reward money, no one would ever have known he was there."

"Brazil." Yona seemed to be deep in thought. "Why did the CIA and FSB go after Reuel?"

"It's part of the deal they made with him." Dmitri pointed to Kelvin.

Kelvin sighed. "I'm just glad they came through. I help them. They help us."

He didn't want to go into details, but it had

taken longer for the Dario and Leonid to do their part of the bargain than it had for Kelvin to help them solve their problems.

"The Gulfstream is fueled," Dmitri told Yona.

"Yes, sir. Could you give us a minute?" Yona asked.

"Sure. Don't take too long. I'll wait for you in the garage. I'm leaving for the airport in twenty minutes with or without you." Dmitri walked away. "Thank you, Kelvin!"

"You're welcome." Kelvin was sure the elderly man could still hear him.

Yona turned to Kelvin. "So you asked me to marry you before you told me about Reuel's capture."

"I wanted to be sure you're marrying me for the right reason."

"For you and not for what you do. Of course." Yona smiled. "We'll talk some more when I get back."

"I'll pray for your safety. And for the team's too."

Yona smiled. "Don't worry. Just make sure you take care of our cat."

Our cat. "Will do."

Poor Mordecai was thirteen years old, and he could be nearing the end of his days on earth. He walked slowly, had stopped chasing rats, preferred to be pampered with soft canned food, and generally looked old.

Kelvin wondered if Mordecai was much older than he looked. After all, he had started out as a stray kitten before he'd moved in with Tereza.

Kelvin prayed that Mordecai would still be alive when Yona returned from her rescue mission, whatever that was. He had learned not to ask questions that he didn't want to hear the answers to.

"Don't get into trouble while I'm gone. I don't want to wait another five years for you to get out of jail." Yona reached for Kelvin. "I don't want to have to explain to our future kids why their dad can't tuck them in at night."

"Future kids?"

"As many as you want." And she gave him one long kiss for the road.

Dear Reader:

I hope you enjoyed reading the story of Kelvin and Yona in *Zero Day*. The next story takes us to a snow-covered mountain of mystery. Dario de la Cruz is involved in this mission, supporting one of

Leland's employees, Iseul Kim, as she tries to rescue her lost brother before he is executed for a crime he might not have committed. This book answers the cybernetics questions in *Zero Sum* and *Zero Day*, as well as takes us to the origins of the Dogs of War in *Once a Spy* (Protector Sweethearts Book 3).

Zero Base (Binary Hackers Book 3)
JanThompson.com/zerobase

Leland Yang-Joule is in ZERO HOUR:

Speaking of Leland, she has traveled across several of my series, including Protector Sweethearts, Defender Sweethearts, and Binary Hackers.

Coming up soon, she will headline her own entire series. Look for the new series prequel, *Zero Hour*, in which we will also see Dmitri and his daughter again, as they work together to help the First Lady of the United States solve an unusual cybercrime.

Zero Hour (A War Hackers Prequel)
JanThompson.com/zerohour

Cayson Yang is in ZERO SUM:

Kelvin's old friend and employer at Binary Systems, Cayson Yang has his own troubles in *Zero Sum*, the first book in the Binary Hackers series, in which he finds himself with cybernetic implants in his head. Will he die? Not if FBI Special Agent Stella Evans does something about it. But can she?

Zero Sum (Binary Hackers Book 1)
JanThompson.com/zerosum

Sign up for my mailing list!

If you like Christian romantic suspense, near-future technothrillers, coastal and beach romance, and romantic women's fiction, feel free to sign up for my mailing list. I'm writing more books for you to enjoy.

JanThompson.com/newsletter

Would you please post a review of this book?

Reviews are very helpful to other readers. If you'd like to leave a review, please follow the link below to reach a retailer site. Thank you very much!

Zero Day (Binary Hackers Book 2)
JanThompson.com/zeroday

Sneak peek...

While waiting for the next book, *Zero Base*, have
you read the first book in Binary Hackers? *Zero
Sum* is the story of Kelvin's employer and friend,
Cayson Yang, in hot trouble with a cybernetic kill
switch implanted in his head. Continue reading for
a sneak peek of Binary Hackers Book 1.

A broken hacker.
A brave FBI agent.
A deadly brain implant.

In *Zero Sum* (Binary Hackers Book 1), FBI Cybercrime Special Agent Stella Evans finds the last surviving computer consultant who holds the key to destroying a terrorist organization's global network, but Cayson Yang may not live long enough to dismantle the computer system.

The Chaos...

Computer network specialist Cayson Yang's struggling network infrastructure company has received a rash of new clients lately, the total income of which finally puts Binary Systems, Inc., in the black for the first time ever. He is now able to give pay raises to himself and his business partner and cousin, Leland Yang-Joule, and bonuses to his employees. Cayson dreams of a bigger office space for them all.

Somewhere between two dollars in his bank account and a two-million-dollar computer network contract, Cayson finds himself in the crosshair of the world's most notorious terrorist organization that is now coming after him, his business partners, his family, and even relatives he doesn't know exist.

Ignoring repeated warning lights might have been Cayson's downfall, but it's too late for him to backtrack...

The Crime...

Assigned to the National Cyber Investigative Joint Task Force, FBI Special Agent Stella Evans finishes assisting her colleagues from the Counterterrorism Division to apprehend a notorious terrorist.

On trial in Europe for war crimes too numerous to list, Molyneux refuses to help the authorities dismantle her sophisticated international computer network. The only alternative is to find the architects of this network and hope they will cooperate.

Shutting down Molyneux's underground computer network is the best way to destroy those mercenary terrorists for hire. However, the terrorist organization doesn't want to be outdone. A successor is named, and they begin to kill off anyone who has worked on the underground network in the past.

The Crisis...

By the time Stella reaches the Binary Systems global headquarters in Atlanta, Georgia, most of the original computer specialists who worked for Molyneux are either dead or have disappeared—except their fearful leader, Cayson Yang, the final link, kept alive for reasons unknown.

Stella finds herself at a crossroad between duty and following Cayson and the cybernetic implants in his head. She stands to lose not only her carefully cultivated career but, more dangerously, her closely guarded heart as she decides what to do with the Pandora's box she has opened.

Zero Sum (Binary Hackers Book 1)
JanThompson.com/zerosum

Binary Hackers
JanThompson.com/binary

To receive book news from Jan Thompson:
JanThompson.com/newsletter

ZERO SUM PROLOGUE SNEAK PEEK

BINARY HACKERS BOOK 1

"This better pay off, Kel," Cayson Yang said when his employee and friend came back to their booth at a corner of the noisy convention center. "We paid five thousand dollars for this spot, and nobody has stopped by all morning. Day two."

All around their tiny booth were gargantuan displays from mega technology firms that Cayson's small computer consulting company could never hope to compete with. They were big, loud, noisy, and they had food. Which Kelvin Gallagher had been munching on as he made the rounds, leaving Cayson to manage the Yottaflops Data Storage LLC booth on his own.

Kelvin had a mouthful of snacks. He muttered something about missing breakfast. It came out sounding like he was missing *butter*.

Or *buffer*, depending on if you were at work or home.

"There must be hundreds of tech expos in the southeast, and we had to pick this one where we're invisible," Cayson continued.

"We? You picked it," Kelvin reminded him.

"Well, I'm scolding myself right now." Cayson pointed to one of the booths nearby. It had a big poster of a bobblehead advertising 3D printing, and a long wraparound line of people. "We're in the wrong business."

Kelvin pulled out something from his pocket. It was a bobblehead doll of himself.

"Whoa. So that's what they're doing over there?" Cayson asked.

"Yeah. You can ask them to print anything for you. The kid in front of me skipped away with a nerf gun that actually shoots darts. I got this." He shook his bobblehead.

"You do have a big head. How much did it cost you?"

Kelvin winked. "If you had to ask, you can't afford it."

Across another aisle, speakers blared loud Bollywood music as a huge crowd gathered around a demonstration of graphics design innovations.

Cayson felt the urge to get off his folding chair and join the decibels of success.

Instead, he found himself tidying up his empty counter, stacking up business cards and a sorry brochure he had printed off their office printer— because someone had forgotten to order new brochures.

We're a digital company. We don't do paper. Save the trees!

The IKEA countertop was slightly chipped on a couple of sides from when he and Kelvin had tried to offload it from the top of his hybrid vehicle on Monday morning. That was after the Atlanta police had given him a citation for dangerous driving.

How was he supposed to know that bungee cords had a breaking point?

His D in college physics hadn't helped.

"Maybe we need a bowl of candy," Kelvin suggested. "Food draws people."

"Candy is not food."

"A technicality." Kelvin downed a whole bottle of soda and smacked his lips. "Maybe it's the name of the company."

"What's wrong with Yottaflops?" Cayson had picked the name of the company carefully.

At this moment in his life, yotta was the largest metric unit.

Hence, *yottaflops.*

A bazillion floating point operations per second.

Ten to the power of twenty-four.

That's some fast server.

"The dichotomy in meanings is too obvious," Kelvin explained, as if he thought that his employer had missed the point. "If we're not talking server speed, but data storage, it should be YottaBytes."

"But we're not only doing data storage," Cayson countered. "We do primarily systems. Systems mean servers, and servers means FLOPS."

Kelvin pointed to the logo on his bright-yellow tee shirt. "This says *Data Storage.*"

"Whatever you do, don't talk to Leland about this. She's been wanting to fold Yottaflops into our parent company, Binary Systems."

"One name to rule them all..."

"She has fifty-one percent of the company shares. If she says it costs too much money to run two separate companies, then that's the way it is." Cayson looked around, wondering where all the customers were. "It has already cost too much money to change everything. Bank cards, logos, door signs, checkbooks—"

"Whoa. What? Did you say checkbooks? Who uses checkbooks these days?"

"I do. And I had them specially printed. A lot of money has gone into this business and we're still not breaking even."

Cayson had sold his house to start Binary Systems, Inc. Then he created a branch to give Kelvin a job. It hadn't seemed ridiculous at first because Cayson felt great saving Kelvin.

Thing is, Cayson was not Kelvin's savior.

But the deed had been done.

Binary Systems had spawned off Yottaflops, and now Cayson owed the IRS money.

The companies had to succeed.

Cayson couldn't live in Mom's basement too long. Pretty soon she would ask him to do more than just take out the trash. At least she had not yet suggested that he volunteer in her law office in exchange for free meals.

Well, she had been taking care of his cats when he was at work all day and night long.

"Whatever," Kelvin said. "It's your company. Say, when is Leland coming? I have to get back to the machine room. Our Dubai client wants his data backed up somewhere safe and offshore."

"Hush."

"Like anyone can hear us—or even cares." Kelvin put up a palm. "Sorry. I didn't mean that in a bad way. Obscurity has its benefits, you know, especially in our line of work."

Cayson said nothing.

"I'll stay if you want me to." Kelvin wadded up another candy wrapper and tossed it into the trash can under the counter.

"I don't think we'll have a lot of foot traffic the rest of the day. Why don't you go?"

"See you at the meeting." Kelvin shook his head. "Who in the world calls for a meeting at three in the morning?"

Guilty as charged.

Well, when the customer was paying half their income, Cayson had no choice but to comply, even if they wanted to talk business at a time convenient to them. It would not always be during the day in Cayson's time zone.

The perks and perils of having global clients.

Cayson watched Kelvin go. He meandered in and out of the booths, picking up snacks, brochures, and such.

Kelvin was a hard worker. Not as brilliant a hacker as Cayson's cousin and business partner, Leland, but he was a great system administrator. And he didn't need any sleep. He could fill in all night long and still function in the daytime.

Boisterous cheering across the aisle from the Bollywood booth made Cayson look that way.

He flinched.

Blocking his view was a ghost from his past.

Startled, Cayson gripped the counter and felt the chipped edge cut into his palm.

He couldn't remember her username. He had only seen her online. Never in person.

Didn't she live in Asia somewhere? Macau someplace?

What was she doing in the United States?

Something must be terribly wrong for her to show up here. Why here? Why now?

"Are you Cayson Yang?" She sounded like she was in a hurry.

Her accent was pretty good. She had said

online that she had learned English by watching American television shows.

But that was eighteen months ago.

No one was supposed to contact anyone else in the team.

They had all agreed.

What is she doing here?

Cayson decided he had to have a talk with Dmitri about this breach of security.

"Who's asking for him?" Cayson replied.

"Do you always speak in third person?"

"Huh?"

"Your name tag says *Cayson Yang*."

"Oh." Cayson winced. *Note to self: stop wearing name tags.*

"How may I help you?" He started over, continuing his charade. *Definitely need to talk with Dmitri about this.*

"I have a warning for Ulysses."

What warning? "You mean a message?"

"A warning."

Only a small handful of people knew who Ulysses was.

And even fewer people knew where he had gone.

In fact, Cayson himself had no idea where Ulysses was at the moment. Only Ulysses's best friend knew, and the latter was incommunicado.

Cayson prayed to God for mercy. He had thought that blighted time in his career had been long gone. How could it resurface now, when he was trying to make a legitimate, above-board living?

"He no longer works for me," he said. "He's off the grid."

Bollywood music thumped in his ears. People cheered and made a lot of noise.

Cayson saw the woman's lips move, but he couldn't hear anything.

She came around the counter.

Cayson felt a sudden splash of spit or liquid or something on his face.

His eyes reflexively shut, and his shoulders pulled back. He lost his balance, and fell backward, going down on the carpeted floor.

As he rolled, he felt a sharp, quick stab just above his left ear.

The pain shot through his skull.

He screamed.

Zero Sum (Binary Hackers Book 1)
JanThompson.com/zerosum

Binary Hackers
JanThompson.com/binary

To receive book news from Jan Thompson:
JanThompson.com/newsletter

ACKNOWLEDGEMENTS

Many thanks to my Georgia Press publishing team for keeping up with my writing schedule.

Thank you to editors Lesley McDaniel and Dori Harrell for copyediting this book, and to Lenda Selph for proofreading this book. I appreciate these professionals and their invaluable hard work.

I am grateful to God for my husband and son for their support and encouragement.

And I'll always remember my beloved mother and my late father for having instilled in me the love of reading and writing from a very early age. I miss my father here on earth, but I will see him in heaven some bright day.

Most of all, I am eternally thankful to my Lord and Savior, Jesus Christ, who died on the cross to save me from my sins and rose again from the grave to give me eternal life. Without Him, I can write nothing (John 15:5).

Jan Thompson
John 3:16

BOOKS BY JAN THOMPSON

CHRISTIAN ROMANTIC SUSPENSE & BEACH ROMANCE

BINARY HACKERS (Near-Future Inspirational Romantic Thrillers)

- Book 1: Zero Sum
- Book 2: Zero Day
- Book 3: Zero Base
- Book 4: Zero Trust

PROTECTOR SWEETHEARTS (Christian Romantic Suspense)

- Book 1: Once a Thief
- Book 2: Once a Hero

- Book 3: Once a Spy
- Book 4: Twice a Fighter
- Book 5: Twice a Convict
- Book 6: Twice a Soldier

DEFENDER SWEETHEARTS (Christian Romantic Suspense)

- Book 1: Never a Traitor
- Book 2: Never a Hostage
- Book 3: Never a Fugitive
- Book 4: Always a Maverick
- Book 5: Always a Champion
- Book 6: Always a Guardian

SAVANNAH SWEETHEARTS (Christian Coastal City & Beach Town Romance)

- Prequel: Ask You Later
- Book 1: Know You More
- Book 2: Tell You Soon (Romance with Suspense)
- Book 3: Draw You Near
- Book 4: Cherish You So
- Book 5: Walk You There

- Book 6: Love You Always (Romance with Suspense)
- Book 7: Kiss You Now
- Book 8: Find You Again
- Book 9: Wish You Joy (Christmas Year Round)
- Book 10: Call You Home

VACATION SWEETHEARTS (Christian Travel Romance)

- Book 1: Smile for Me
- Book 2: Reach for Me (Romance with Suspense)
- Book 3: Wait for Me (Romance with Suspense)
- Book 4: Look for Me (Romance with Suspense)
- Book 5: Pray for Me
- Book 6: Care for Me
- Book 7: Cheer for Me

SEASIDE CHAPEL (Christian Small Town Beach Romance)

- Book 1: His Longing Heart (second edition of Share with Me)
- Book 2: His Wake-Up Call (second edition of Step with Me)
- Book 3: His Morning Kiss (previously published as Sing with Me)
- Book 4: His Quiet Serenade
- Book 5: His Waiting Love
- Book 6: His Beach Retreat

Subscribe to Jan Thompson's mailing list: JanThompson.com/newsletter

BINARY HACKERS

Like more suspense with your Christian romance? Like to read suspense thrillers? If you're looking for clean near-future romantic suspense without compromising the Christian faith, these books are for you.

From *USA Today* bestselling author Jan Thompson come these inspirational near-future cyberthrillers combining technothriller and romance, starting with Binary Hackers that feature computer specialists living at the edge of cyberspace, where they have to juggle being law-abiding truth-telling Christians while carrying out their assignments by any and all means possible.

The Binary Hackers series is set in the same story world as Jan's other books, and characters from the other series may make cameo appearances in this series and vice versa.

JanThompson.com/binary

- Book 1: Zero Sum
- Book 2: Zero Day
- Book 3: Zero Base
- Book 4: Zero Trust

PROTECTOR SWEETHEARTS

Private investigator Helen Hu and her associates specialize in searching for missing persons and hunting for lost treasures. Join them in their adventure suspense around the world in *USA Today* bestselling author Jan Thompson's Protector Sweethearts, a series of Christian Romantic Suspense with a side of mystery. Protector Sweethearts is a spin-off of Savannah Sweethearts and Vacation Sweethearts.

JanThompson.com/protector

- Book 1: Once a Thief

- Book 2: Once a Hero
- Book 3: Once a Spy
- Book 4: Twice a Fighter
- Book 5: Twice a Convict
- Book 6: Twice a Soldier

DEFENDER SWEETHEARTS

Defender Sweethearts is a sister series to the Protector Sweethearts Christian romantic suspense collection. While the heroes in Protector Sweethearts search for lost treasures and lost people, the Defender Sweethearts novels focus on protecting the helpless and hopeless. The main characters in Defender Sweethearts come from the supporting cast in Protector Sweethearts.

JanThompson.com/defender

- Book 1: Never a Traitor

- Book 2: Never a Hostage
- Book 3: Never a Fugitive
- Book 4: Always a Maverick
- Book 5: Always a Champion
- Book 6: Always a Guardian

SAVANNAH SWEETHEARTS

Welcome to the new south! From *USA Today* bestselling author Jan Thompson come these clean and wholesome, sweet and inspirational Christian romances set on the romantic beaches of Tybee Island and in the coastal town of Savannah, Georgia.

Meet a group of multiracial and multiethnic churchgoing Christians who love the Lord, work hard in their careers, and seek God's will for their love lives. Against a backdrop of ocean, sand, and sun, these inspirational romances showcase aspects of the human need for God and for one another. Have some tea, settle in a comfortable reading chair, and enjoy these sweet celebrations of faith, hope, and love in Jesus Christ.

JanThompson.com/savannah

- Prequel: Ask You Later
- Book 1: Know You More
- Book 2: Tell You Soon (Romance with Suspense)
- Book 3: Draw You Near
- Book 4: Cherish You So
- Book 5: Walk You There
- Book 6: Love You Always (Romance with Suspense)
- Book 7: Kiss You Now
- Book 8: Find You Again
- Book 9: Wish You Joy (Christmas Year Round)
- Book 10: Call You Home

VACATION SWEETHEARTS

Travel with our friends from Savannah, Georgia, to the coast and to the mountains. Cheer them on as they celebrate the immeasurable grace and undeserved mercy of God through Jesus Christ.

The Vacation Sweethearts novels are a spin-off of Jan's Savannah Sweethearts series, and fans will recognize familiar faces from Riverside Chapel, a church in the coastal city of Savannah, Georgia. In fact, we might even visit the beach town of Tybee Island from time to time to visit old friends and beloved families...

JanThompson.com/vacation

- Book 0 (Prequel): Time for Me
- Book 1: Smile for Me (International Romance)
- Book 2: Reach for Me (Romance with Suspense)
- Book 3: Wait for Me (Romance with Suspense)
- Book 4: Look for Me (Romance with Suspense)
- Book 5: Pray for Me (International Romance)
- Book 6: Care for Me
- Book 7: Cheer for Me (International Romance)

SEASIDE CHAPEL

Welcome to *USA Today* bestselling author Jan Thompson's Seaside Chapel Christian beach romance series. These novels are set on real-life St. Simon's Island, Georgia—a beach town where history is all around and the future is a moment away—and the neighboring fictitious Seaside Island, where the rich and famous live.

Savor the small-town atmosphere and the warm southern beaches of St. Simon's Island and the idyllic Golden Isles along the Atlantic Ocean. Enjoy the music of the orchestra and hymns of the church, and hang out with our Christian friends who attend Seaside Chapel, a little church by the sea known for its beach weddings and fair share of love and life.

As these Christians grow in their knowledge and understanding of God, they are tested in their spiritual maturity, their love lives, and their relationships with others. Share their heartaches and healing, and cheer them on as they celebrate faith, family, and friends.

JanThompson.com/seaside

- Book 1: His Longing Heart (second edition of Share with Me)
- Book 2: His Wake-Up Call (second edition of Step with Me)
- Book 3: His Morning Kiss (previously published as Sing with Me)
- Book 4: His Quiet Serenade
- Book 5: His Waiting Love
- Book 6: His Beach Retreat

ABOUT JAN THOMPSON

USA Today bestselling author Jan Thompson writes clean and wholesome contemporary Christian romance with elements of women's fiction, Christian romantic suspense with an air of mystery, and inspirational international thrillers with threads of sweet Christian romance. Jan's books are for readers who love inspiring stories of faith, hope, and love in Jesus Christ.

Raised on a tropical island in the eastern hemisphere, Jan now lives and writes in the western hemisphere. Her international background gives her a unique multicultural and multiracial perspective to her novels and books. The island has never left her, and she reminisces about beach life in her beach romance novels.

When Jan is not busy writing small-town stories, she writes big-city romantic suspense and international technothrillers, a nod to her previous career in computer science. She weaves technology with human interests, reflecting the current and future digital world. And romance. There's always romance.

Beyond the printed page, Jan is a wife, mother, family scribe, avid reader, occasional artist, erstwhile pianist, and chief of staff to the family cat.

Find out more about Jan Thompson:
JanThompson.com

Subscribe to Jan's book news mailing list:
JanThompson.com/newsletter

For God so loved the world,
that He gave His only begotten Son,
that whosoever believeth in Him should not perish,
but have everlasting life.
—John 3:16

www.ingramcontent.com/pod-product-compliance
Lightning Source LLC
Chambersburg PA
CBHW020755250626
47155CB00003B/1091